To my sons who never stopped encouraging me to write these stories.

To the men who worked in the woods and on the lakes and rivers, and especially to those who died there so we could read our newspapers every day.

Cover design and illustrations by Taylore Aussiker.

Printed in the United States of America
First Printing, June 2019
ISBN 1-7339153-0-4
'Suncookers LLC, publisher
Suncookersworld.com

Tanglefoot

Author's Note

Chesuncook Lake and Village really exist. Most place names and geography are accurate, but I have created a work of fiction that echoes real characters I knew and real events that took place in the Northwoods of Maine.

Most of the story was written in a small cabin on the shore of the lake with the hotel (which really did burn in March of 2018, having stood for 165 years) within sight.

The Native American stories and tribal customs (Eastern Abenaki tribes) are only a reflection of the originals, and in some cases wholly imagined.

Whiskey making did occur in the Village before, during and after prohibition.

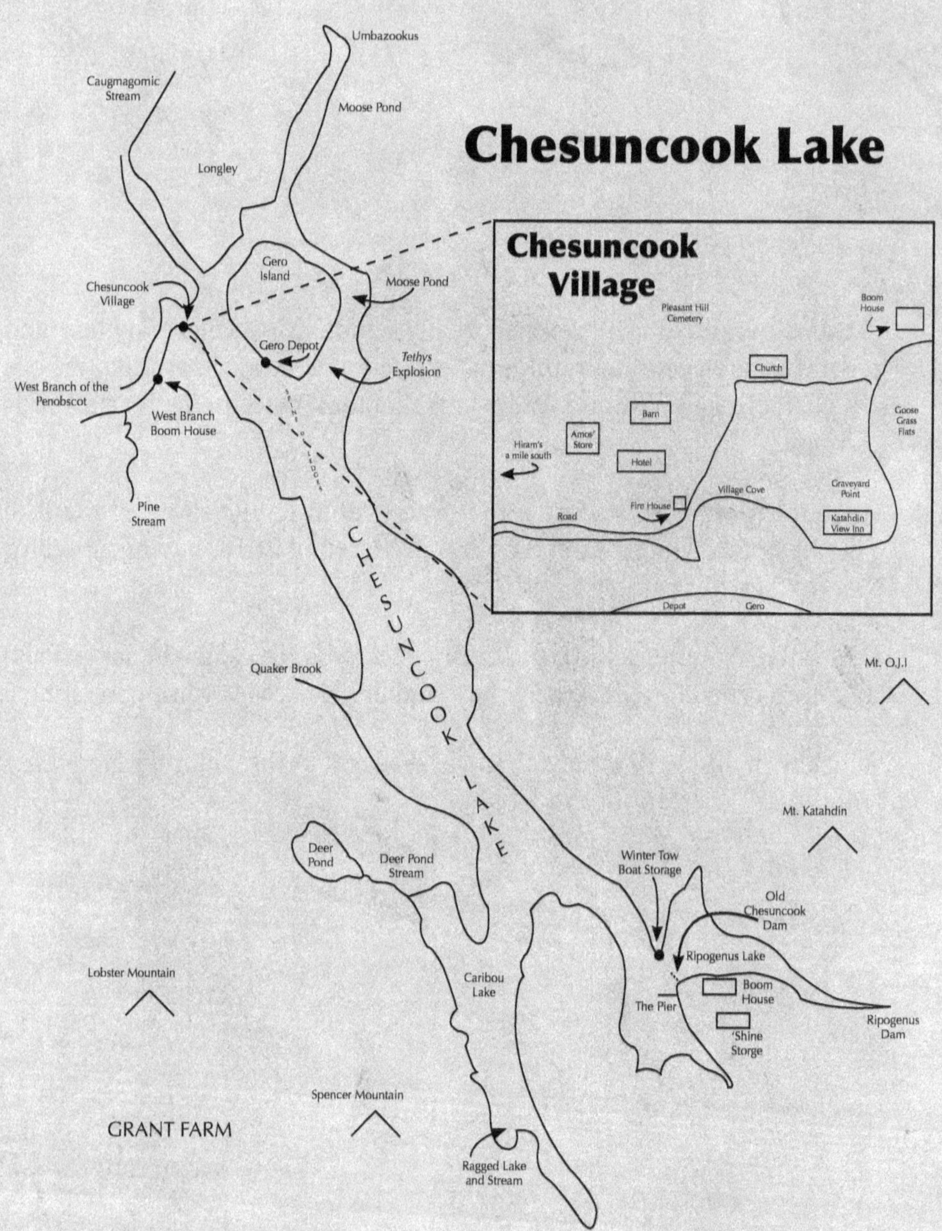

Chesuncook Lake

Umbazookus
Caugmagomic Stream
Moose Pond
Longley
Gero Island
Moose Pond
Chesuncook Village
Gero Depot
Tethys Explosion
West Branch of the Penobscot
West Branch Boom House
Pine Stream
Quaker Brook
CHESUNCOOK LAKE
Deer Pond
Deer Pond Stream
Caribou Lake
Lobster Mountain
Spencer Mountain
GRANT FARM
Ragged Lake and Stream
Mt. O.J.I
Mt. Katahdin
Winter Tow Boat Storage
Old Chesuncook Dam
Ripogenus Lake
The Pier
Boom House
'Shine Storge
Ripogenus Dam

Chesuncook Village

Pleasant Hill Cemetery
Boom House
Church
Barn
Amos' Store
Hotel
Hiram's a mile south
Goose Grass Flats
Village Cove
Graveyard Point
Fire House
Road
Katahdin View Inn
Depot   Gero

SIXTEEN WOODSMEN DROWNED IN MAINE Motorboat on Chesuncook Lake Takes Fire and They Tried to Swim to Shore.
BANGOR, Me., Nov. 19--Sixteen woodsmen were drowned in Chesuncook Lake, in the heart of the lumbering district, late yesterday afternoon when a motorboat took fire. The men were being taken across the lake from Chesuncook Dam to Cuxabesis.

Efforts to extinguish the fire failing, the party became panic-stricken and many leaped overboard, according to word brought here today. The icy water soon exhausted those who tried to escape by swimming, and all of them are believed to have lost their lives. About half the crew remained with the boat, and, although they were forced to drop overboard after the engine stopped, they clung to the side of the craft until it was blown shoreward by the strong wind.

The boat drifted against a mass of stumps which protruded above the water and these served as isles of safety for the men until they were rescued by crews from neighboring lumber camps and village folks who had seen the flames from a distance.

Seventeen in all are believed to have been saved. Some of these, however, were reported in a serious condition from exposure.

When word was sent here seven bodies had been removed, of which four had been identified. They were John Zorrill, P. C. McCaul and John McDowell, all of Notham, P.E.I., and Arthur O'Connor, residence unknown.

Because of the large number of lumbermen being sent into the woods at this season it was said that it would be difficult, if not impossible, to learn the names of the missing ones, except through identification of bodies recovered.

(The New York Times, New York, NY 20 Nov 1920)

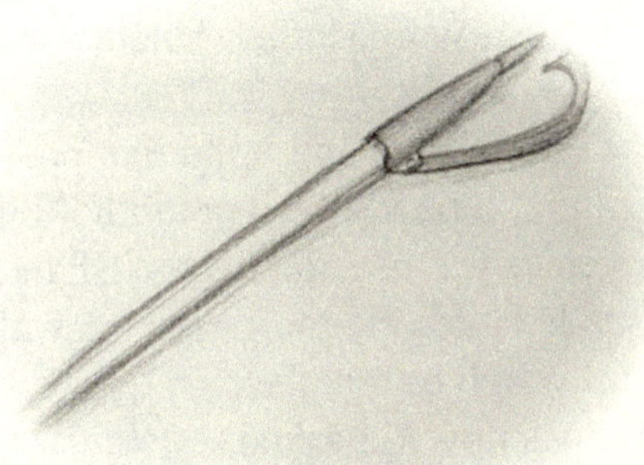

Chapter 1

When I turned 14, I became a smuggler. After thirty-five years, I've made a lot of money, and I'm still at it, but can't shake the memories of the tragic costs that are always part of an illegal business.

It was 1920, and I went to work for my father who ran a boat carrying Company woodsmen, mostly immigrants and supplies, mostly the Company's. I was expected to step up and shoulder my share of this new family business, making and running whiskey down river in the face of the new Prohibition laws. I was old enough, Father told me, to work beside him and his brother, my Uncle Amos. I was his only son since my older brothers Will and Sam went to fight in the Great War but remained in France. Their gravestones are here in our little cemetery; their bodies are somewhere under the grass in a farmer's field in Verdun.

"Hey, Charlie," Uncle Amos greeted me as I came into the barn. He was, among other things, our village blacksmith, and this morning he was getting ready to re-shoe our pair of oxen, Lightning and Thunder.

"Hi, Uncle Amos. Father said I should come out to help." Father was always instructing me to do one thing or another, but I really liked working in the barn. The scent of the hay, the animals, and this morning the smell of iron being heated up in the forge had greeted me as I walked between the big sliding doors.

Built by Bob Cunningham in 1860, our giant barn loomed over the lake. You could see the cupola and eagle-topped weather vane half way to the Dam, some miles away. It was a landmark we strained to see on those foggy, rainy boat rides while ferrying cargo and woodsmen up and down the lake. On the lake shore and surrounded on three sides by vast fields, the barn was home to dozens of horses, our oxen Thunder and Lightning, some sheep, a sty full of pigs and a dozen laying hens. It was the heart of our village. Neighbors would stop by for blacksmith work, help with a lame horse, or just to visit with Mother, Uncle Amos or Father.

"You can bring Thunder over here. Just tie him up to that post." Uncle Amos motioned to a huge beam that looked like it could hold up the whole barn by itself. I headed over to the pen the "boys" shared, clipped a lead to Thunder and persuaded the one-ton critter to walk closer to the forge area. I kept a careful watch on my feet.

"Are you putting on summer shoes now?" I asked.

"It's time," Uncle Amos replied. "The ice has been gone for a couple of weeks, and they'll need the right shoes for spring ploughing and stump pulling." Unlike horses, oxen had split hooves meaning they had two halves of a "shoe" on each foot. They could out-pull horses and would thrive on the poorest growing field without expensive grains. Uncle Amos had raised them from month-old bulls. We had the only pair in our little village, a remote logging community at the north end of Chesuncook Lake.

Calling ourselves "'Suncookers," there were seventy-five of us, and we lived in some forty cabins and houses sited around the fields and lake shore at the north end of the lake. Our village wasn't easy to get to. It took a boat ride up the lake, a canoe trip down the river, or a day long hike over a winter's logging trace to get here. Whichever route the traveler chose, the distance was the same: twenty miles.

In back of our hotel, there was a little building used for a community store. We had regular mail delivery (twice a week in the winters by sleigh, three times in the summers by boat), and our own school, church and town hall all stuffed into one building.

A bare, galvanized coated copper wire connected each home that had a Western Electric hand crank wall phone. We were linked to all the logging camps and the outside world through the switchboard at the Grant Farm. Trucks and cars were brought in on the ice. Sometimes whole camps and a house or two were hauled here on the frozen lake. I remember seeing Thunder and Lightning drag the old town hall away from the lakeshore over the field to its new location up the little hill beside the church. It took four days to ice down the road, but it took only two hours for the "boys" to relocate the building. Mt. Katahdin, the mile-high peak in the center of a large range, filled the southern horizon. The local Indians believed their "Great Spirit" of the same name lived there in the clouds.

The fishing was good at the mouths of those little streams where the trout loved to swim in the cold, spring-fed water. Berries were plentiful in season, and we grew potatoes, beans, squash and corn. You could make a good living fur-trapping if you wanted. It was Eden.

We lived in the Company's hotel, which my family ran. It was huge and painted a light yellow. A gallon of the original paint choice had to be cut by three gallons of white, it was so yellow. It took forty-eight gallons and my brother Will's entire last summer to change the color from white. I know how many gallons it took because I helped carry the paint to the scaffold where he was painting the third floor. I really miss him, and Sam, too. They'd take me fishing for perch, and sometimes we'd catch lake trout off the village pier.

"Here, help steady his leg," Uncle Amos asked me. He had Thunder's lower leg between his, but he needed a hand keeping the upper leg still while he removed the old shoes. This was a job I remember seeing Will and Sam help with. I see them everywhere I go and during every chore I finish.

"Do you think the government will ever find Will and Sam and send what's left of them back home?" I asked.

"Doubt they're even looking. The telegram your folks got mentioned something about a 'mass grave.'"

Just then, Father swaggered into the barn. His short stature and barrel chest made his profile in the bright sun unmistakable. I watched his expression change as he heard Uncle Amos' reply to my question.

"Damned government sent them off to die," he said a bit louder than necessary. It looked like we were in for another one of his tirades against Uncle Sam. "Old men make the wars and then send young men away from their families to die in them. Damn them. All we got back was that telegram from the Adjutant General. I don't think it had twenty words in it. 'Sorry to inform you,' my ass." It was a very short tirade for Father, but maybe it was because he had another thought he needed to share.

"The still you have in the back room, Amos. Is it all set to go?" Father asked.

"Yup, it's all set. Why, running low in the White Lightning department, are you?"

"A little, but I've been thinking," Father mused.

"That could be dangerous," Uncle Amos quipped, placing another iron shoe in the forge's flames.

"Why don't you keep that tongue of yours still a moment, unless you don't want to make a pile of money real easy," Father shot back.

"Money is always good. We're going to need a pile of it after the logs we cut last winter hung up in Caucmagomic Stream." A month ago, as the rivers were opening up after a cold winter, all the wood, every single log of that winter's labor, hung up in the river bed for lack of water to flush them down to the lake. They wouldn't be any good now that the bugs were in them. It was a total loss. Father and Uncle Amos just left them there to rot and walked away, but there was the little matter of paying the cutting crews, the stumpage fees and the supplies they used. It seemed there was never enough money in this family.

"I have a plan that will make us rich!" Father exclaimed with a certain amount of pride.

"Oh, like the gold mine disaster, is it?" Uncle Amos taunted. Now he was in trouble. Father hated to hear that story. I know, I saw his reaction once before when Uncle Amos brought it up. Now I could see his brow furrow. Uncle Amos grabbed the tongs and began to hammer on the red-hot ox shoe.

Father and Uncle Amos were prospecting in Canada when they discovered a rich vein of gold ore. They staked the claim and took the sample to the assay office to do the analysis and the paper work to make the claim legal. When they got back to the site two days later, they found that another prospector had set up his own camp and was digging away on their claim. Father and Uncle Amos were furious. The claim jumper refused to leave, claiming the spot had been his for years. They went back to town to find a Mounty, and they managed to bring back two of them. As the conversation became heated, which didn't take long, Father picked up a shovel and swung it at the claim jumper. The jumper ducked, but the shovel kept going, striking the side of one Mounty's head with the flat of the blade, killing him instantly. Father narrowly escaped jail time since the judge was easily bought. He was forbidden to return to Canada under the threat of a lengthy imprisonment. That experience seemed to have taught him a valuable lesson: enough money in the right hands could make the law leave you alone.

"Someday, Amos, you're going to bring that up, and it'll be the side of your own head that meets a shovel blade!" Of course, Father didn't mean it. He did bark pretty loud, though.

"Then what's the plan, Caleb? I'm all ears." Uncle Amos had stopped grinning.

"We add more stills to the back room and go into production of the best moonshine this pitiful state has ever seen. We'll brand it and sell it to a distributor who'll keep his mouth shut. We'll pay off the sheriff and his deputies to grease the way." National prohibition had been in force since the first of the year, and folks had found their way to their friendly bootlegger and speakeasy. Maine had banned the sale of alcohol for the last fifty years anyway, so there wasn't much of a change here. In our isolated village, moonshine had always been the only alcohol, legal or not. Few could afford the 'real' thing. Besides the law, the Company prohibited the transportation of whiskey up the lake to the logging camps. The men who worked there were way too thirsty.

"When I went to town before the lake froze last December, I got acquainted with Big Mike Matisse. He runs 'The Bearded Lady' on State Street. We plan to meet again to iron out the details. He'll buy all the Tanglefoot we can make."

"Sounds promising," Uncle Amos agreed. "And you're telling me you know how to make the really good stuff?"

"I don't, but there's someone on their way here who can help. Know the name Dan Call? He used to be a preacher before he got into the whiskey making business." Father offered.

"Can't say I've heard of him. A preacher? Who is this guy? Does he pray over the still or something?"

"He's the man," Father sighed, "who started Jack Daniels, that smooth Tennessee whiskey you like so much but can never afford? He's going to help us with the recipe and the still set up. He owes me a favor for supplying him with potatoes so he could make vodka when grain was scarce years ago during a drought. I'll be bringing him up the lake as well as the supplies we need on tomorrow's trip."

I was hoping that Father needed a helping hand loading cargo or something, so I could go along. Boat rides to the Dam and back were a lot of fun. Father would let me steer sometimes, and when the weather was good, I could hang over the front deck and watch the lake pass by, reflections of the clouds and blue sky dissolving into the waves from the V of the bow. Time seemed to pass quickly as I stared at the water.

"I know where I can get two more copper hot water tanks." Uncle Amos dunked another hot iron shoe in a bucket of water to cool it down. "We'll have the materials we need by the time you get back, and I'll have at least one more still ready to run."

Father just nodded, spun on his heel, and walked back to the hotel on another mission. He was probably going to ask Mother for a fresh cup of coffee. That left me with Uncle Amos.

"Come on, Charlie, steady Thunder's leg, for heaven's sake. It's going to take all day to get this little job done if we don't get going. If Will and Sam were with us, we'd be done by now." Father was bitter, but Uncle Amos seemed more practical when it came to my late brothers.

....

The hotel that my family managed had a wrap-around screened-in porch that kept the skeeters away. On some days, it didn't pay to go outside without being coated in bear grease. Hungry flies could suck you dry and chew you to pieces in an hour, there seemed to be so many of them some days.

Mother was the cook, and Father the master guide and transporter. They ran the place for the Company first, and then for our family, tolerating flatlanders who wanted to follow Henry David Thoreau's trip down the West Branch from Moosehead's Northeast Carry via Greenville and Kineo. Once, we had the soda monarch of New York, Henry Zeigler, who brought a dozen friends with him for "Camp Zeigler" they called it. Father had to arrange for a half-dozen guides to get them down the lake to Bangor, a five-day paddle. They wanted to see the pines, wilderness giants that had towered 150 feet over the lake shore and river banks before they were all cut to satisfy Bangor's thirst for lumber. These Thoreau followers were about eighty years too late. That didn't seem to have mattered, as they kept coming just the same.

I spent my days that summer working the stills Uncle Amos had cobbled together. Often, I went down the lake with Father, helping him make a delivery to some waiting trucks. On the return trip up the lake, there would be twenty cases of empty Moxie bottles that sat nearest the wheelhouse where my father kept a close eye on them as he brought the *Tethys* (teth.ease) back to the village. None of the passengers on board ever noticed that the bottles were empty. If they did, no one ever said. Those Moxie bottles wouldn't be empty for long.

....

The next morning, Father called up the stairs.

"Charlie, get cleaned up, pack a change of clothes, and meet me outside in thirty minutes. We're going to town." The new road to Greenville had finally dried out enough so our truck wouldn't sink out of sight in the mud holes. I got my things together, and raced down the stairs, ducking my six-foot frame under the stairway header just in time before whacking my forehead again. I think the hotel was built for 'wee folk.'

Father's words were not suggestions. I never should have asked,

"Where are we going?" on our walk to the boat, but I couldn't seem to stop myself.

"Instead of asking so many questions, Charlie, you need to think more. People who ask questions all the time like you do aren't looked on as particularly smart."

I stung from his verbal rebuke for the rest of the day. He didn't like to be questioned.

What I learned on that trip down river and back set me on a path I have walked ever since, smuggling people and guns instead of moonshine. There's a lot of money in the business, and I'm good at it, having learned from my father, Caleb King, and his partner and brother, my Uncle Amos.

And what I also learned on that season's last trip was that a dead man was a heavy weight.

Chapter 2

By the time I got my suitcase packed, Father was waiting for me in front of the hotel on the veranda. He usually sat in one of the new green wicker chairs facing Mt. Katahdin, or "Big Hill," if you want the Abanaki translation. It was the home of the great spirit, Katahdin. Our end of the Eastern Appalachian Range stretched along the horizon from where the trail to Duck Pond cut into the woods in back of Gero and ended where Red Brook emptied into the lake.

Katahdin was our weather maker. Father told me that most of the village could predict the weather by how the clouds circled around it. I remember seeing the men standing about, talking and gesturing while looking at the sky. One day there'd be horsetail clouds, and another day thunderheads. There were our own quaint names like "scooters" or "ox tails." Wind direction was always changing. It took a while, but I began to figure it out. If there was a south wind, it was going to rain for three days starting pretty soon.

Soon, we'd be heading down the lake, looking at the Abol slide, OJI, Doubletop and Sourbungee, all part of that huge range of glacier ground granite. The lake was fairly calm. Maybe Father would let me take her helm.

Mother was sitting beside him, and I overheard their conversation as I came down the hallway, pausing a moment before approaching the door.

"I don't think this is a good idea, Caleb," I heard Mother say. "There might be others who won't accept the presence of another supplier."

"If we could make as much money doing something else, we would," Father asserted. "This family is in debt. We have no money to get us through another winter, and we have no prospects for earning any except the pittance the Company pays us. What do you propose we do?"

"I don't know, Caleb." Mother smoothed out her apron. "I worry about the consequences."

"Grace, there won't be any," he said. "We'll have more money than you can imagine. We can pay all our debts, buy the hotel the Company has offered us, and maybe that potato farm in the County. We won't be wanting for anything."

I don't think I had ever heard Mother disagree with Father before. What surprised me was his calm manner. Usually, he raised his voice if anyone questioned him, but not now. I came out onto the porch and set my suitcase down.

"I'm ready when you are." I put my bag on the floor, smiling with anticipation of a boat ride down the lake.

"Let's go, Charlie," Father ordered. I said goodbye to Mother as we left the porch. "Be a good boy," she said as she handed me a paper sack of warm sugar donuts and gave me a hug. Father and I walked by the giant white birch tree that spread over the lawn, down the narrow pea stone path to our dock, and loaded ourselves in the *Tethys*. I didn't know what was ahead of us in Bangor. I do know that it wasn't long before we finished the last of the donuts.

Open both in the back and on the sides, the *Tethys'* wheelhouse was nothing more than a steering wheel with two cables to the rudder. A front enclosure of small windows extended two feet on each side. There were manually operated wipers for those rainy days or when the wind whipped the wave's spray over the top of the cabin. A little handle went through the window molding and connected to a wiper blade. Turning the handle moved the wiper. A green painted canvas roof, curved at the center to shed the rain and spray, extended from the tops of the windows across the entire width and ran all the way back to the stern, supported by evenly spaced mahogany posts. Passengers and cargo stowed under the canopy were well protected from sun and spray on both her sides and stern.

"Throw off the bow line," Father shouted at me after he started the engine. I did as he asked, and then walked to the stern that faced the lake, anticipating his next command.

"Untie the stern," he bellowed, and just as I was about to unwrap the rope from the cleat, a rather disheveled man carrying a large grey and tattered canvas duffle ran over the dock for a ride down the lake with us.

"Wait up," he called out as he stepped onto the dock. Throwing his duffle to me first, he then hopped aboard. I untied the stern, Father backed the *Tethys* away from the dock, turned her bow down the lake, and we were off.

This last-minute passenger was a river driver who had had enough of that dangerous work, cashed out, and wanted a ride back to civilization. We weren't too surprised to see a last-minute passenger anxious to escape the poor conditions of the logging camps. His spiked boots were draped over his shoulder by their leather laces, a greasy red bandanna hung from his back pocket, and he wore a cap similar to the ones I had seen other drivers wear. I could see a pulp pick and an ax handle sticking out of his duffle. I sure hoped he got a soaking bath when we got to town, and I cringed every time he scratched his head, pulling something out of his hair. It took most of the trip back up the lake the next day for his stink to leave the boat.

"I feel sorry for those poor bastards who have to stay to work off their debt," the driver asserted. "If I hadn't brought my own gear, I'd be stuck." The Company charged their workers for everything, every meal, every pair of socks and every night's rest in the over-crowded and vermin infested bunk houses. By the time the drive was over, their pay was barely enough to last a month living in the outside world. A few ended up owing the Company at the end of the season.

"I sure hope the roads are passable to Greenville," complained our passenger. Father looked at him and then turned away. It was the last thing he said the entire trip as he relaxed on the padded stern seat. One thing Father couldn't stand was a chatty rider, and he could quiet most people with just a look.

I was hoping the roads were good, too. This was pretty exciting for me. I hadn't been to Bangor for some time. Arriving at a washed-out bridge might be the only warning that a trip could not be completed. Making deliveries could be challenging when beavers had been busy building dams that flooded out the trace. Traces, primitive paths for hauling pulp wood, were mostly for winter use. Snow would fill in the low spots and make it passable for the horse and sled. A few of these primitive roads could be used in the summer if it hadn't rained much, but most were just open swaths through an uncharted forest.

The Company had built a new "all weather" road to the Dam just a few years ago to haul cement, equipment, and materials for what became the largest private dam in the world, one hundred feet high and two thousand feet across at Ripogenus Gorge. Horses and oxen pulled the heavy loads from Lily Bay Landing on Moosehead. The old Chesuncook Dam we were headed for, a few miles upstream, was now well under water. We only called it "the Dam." That was where we tied the *Tethys* at the Company's pier.

"Charlie, you'd better get the bow and stern lines ready," Father shouted to me. I was still hanging off the bow watching the lake peel away from the clapboarded sides of the *Tethys*.

The pier we were heading for was now in sight. The low water made it seem pretty high, but a floating dock right beside it made it easy to load and unload, using a gangplank to the rocky shoreline. Just before we brushed the edge of the dock, Father shouted, "Get on the stern line, Charlie." He brought us right beside the tie-up, and I jumped out, the boat still moving, wrapping the stern line around the cleat, nearly stopping us short. As I ran for the bow, the floating dock moving a little with the attached *Tethys*, Father tossed me that line, and I pulled the bow in closer. Bumpers were already dangling from the side, cushioning the *Tethys* from banging on the float.

The *West Branch*, a crude oil burner, was tied up at the end of the pier. Fuel was flowing through the large galvanized pipes that ran from several huge tanks on the hill down to the end of the pier. The smell of "Bunker C" was nearly overpowering. We didn't take long to secure the *Tethys*. Father shut the engine off and locked the cabin door.

"Let's get our gear and get the truck." Father jumped on the float. I grabbed my pack, the passenger took his duffle, and we walked up the little rise to the garage where we kept our new 1919 Oldsmobile Model T Economy truck. Its long cargo area was covered with canvas roll ups for the sides and back. Father started it up, and soon we were on our way, the truck's body rattling as we rolled through an endless sea of pot holes. Our passenger rode in the back, sitting on one of the benches under the canvas cover. Thank goodness there was no room for him in the cab.

We gassed up in Greenville, then Dover, and made the last two hours to Bangor without a flat or a breakdown. None of the roads were tarred then, even ones in Bangor, although there were a few cobblestone streets where the rich folk lived on outer Hammond. When we parked in front of the Exchange Hotel, our passenger hopped out of the back without a word of thanks, practically running to an alley's back door, seeming to disappear through the brick wall. Father opened the truck's door. "I've got to order supplies from the Mercantile. You can help load."

I followed Father to the Bangor Mercantile. In the store's window, hanging from some rope, was a red Iver Johnson bicycle. It was a store model, meaning it had heavier wheel rims, frame and center crank, perfect for the poor roads in our village. That bicycle was second on my wish list. First was a Winchester model 1897 sixteen-gauge shotgun, perfect for fall bird hunting. Both were beyond my means, but a boy could dream.

"Come on, Charlie. We've got things to do." I had stopped in front of the store window admiring the bike. "Don't let me forget the Crystal White Soap and Dr. Kilmer's Swamp Root Elixir for Mother," Father instructed me. He then handed a list to the grocer behind a long counter while a stock boy set out several wooden boxes to hold some of the supplies. I picked out a side of bacon, and Father asked the clerk to add the soap and elixir Mother wanted.

While I was loading bags of sugar, corn and burlap sacks of dried fruit, I watched cars, trucks, horses and wagons scoot by. It was a nice late spring day, and a lot of folks were out. Some ladies with parasols were hanging out at the corner just ahead, talking and laughing with the men who stopped to say hello. Some walked off together, coming my way, and then disappeared into the hotel. I remember thinking they seemed really friendly.

In an hour's time, the supplies were loaded and there was no more room in the back of the truck. Cases of empty Moxie bottles were surrounded by piles of supplies. Father started the engine, and we made our way to the bottom of State Street where he pulled over, then backed into a little alley. He stopped the motor and turned to me.

"Charlie, you have an important job on this trip and I'm going to depend on you to watch my back."

"Okay," I said, waiting for the rest of the instructions that were sure to come. I had no idea what he meant at the time.

"When we go in," he began, "follow me closely but look around for any suspicious characters. Take note of who they're looking at, especially if they're looking at us. Don't stare, but glance around the room from time to time. Got it?"

"I got it," I said. I was good at remembering faces at least. Maybe that's the reason I was brought along, I wondered.

We stepped out of the truck and walked down the dead-end alley between two tall buildings, one a hardware store and the other a branch of Bangor Savings. There, near the end of the alley, was a low wooden door at the bottom of a few steps. As we got closer, the smell of urine stung my nose. Father knocked three times, paused, then rapped the brass knocker two more times. A small window in the upper part of the door slid open behind a wire mesh.

"Caleb King to see Mike Matisse," Father whispered. The window slid closed and a few moments passed. I looked around while we waited and saw a thin man standing in the shadow of the doorway on the other side of the alley, near the center. I couldn't see his face, but I did see his floppy hat with the eagle feather in its band. That I would remember.

"Father, there's someone standing in the doorway behind us."

"Alright." Father looked down the alley over my shoulder. "Turn around once in a while to see if he moves and let me know if he does." Father touched his right hip where I knew he kept his revolver. He used it mostly to scare off bears, I thought, but I got the feeling there was something even more dangerous here.

My stomach began to tighten up, hair rose a bit along my neck, and just when I began praying for the door in front of us to open, it did just that. As we went inside, I scanned the alley one last time. The man with the feather had disappeared. We stepped through the doorway, even Father ducking his short frame, and the next thing I knew we were in a bar.

Inside I saw the dark wood of the bar, the dark stained chairs and tables and a few electric lights on the walls. Everything seemed so murky. Large, polished brass spittoons were at each end of the bar, and one was near the door. The place smelled of sour beer and old cigars. There were a few people at the tables drinking while a slot machine in the corner clacked and rang as the man we had just brought down from the village threw away his hard-earned pay. He had cleaner clothes, a haircut, and seemed to sway about as he fumbled for more change in his pockets. He had a "snoot full," as Mother would say.

The bar was one long plank of pine, varnished bark still on the edge. There wasn't a mirror behind the entire length, but there was one behind a few short and recessed shelves of pretty bottles in the center, set into the wall. At the top of the recess, I could see the bottom part of a large painting that could be pulled down to hide them in case the liquor control boys paid an unexpected visit, having chopped down the thick wooden door.

There were no windows. A few light bulbs in a forest green metal cover hung over the pool table, a crystal chandelier was over one of the tables, and a few lights hung over the bar. The pool balls were neatly arranged on a wall rack with a dark wood cue holder beside it. On the rails of the green felt table were inlaid diamonds of ivory. A blue block of cue chalk rested on each side. The pockets were knitted like snowshoe webbing with little tassels hanging beneath them. What supported the table was the most interesting: a group of cast iron lions, side by side. That table was never going to move easily, that's for sure.

Two doors were along the back wall. While I was looking around, I saw the thin man who had been hanging out in the alley while we were waiting to be admitted. He came in from the door at the left and sat at the bar. The bartender poured him some whiskey, left the bottle, and came over to us.

"Have a seat over there," he said as he pointed to a corner table. "Mike will be over in a minute." The bartender headed back to wait on a couple that had come in after us.

"Keep a sharp eye, Charlie." Father moved toward the corner table, and I was right on his heels. "Don't get distracted like you're apt to. Sit beside me while we wait for Mike." I was so mesmerized by things I had seen only in a magazine, I nearly forgot to check out the thin guy with the feather in his hat band. Without staring, I got a better look at his face. I caught a glimpse of a nasty scar from the end of his nose, curving down, then up across his right cheek to his ear. It looked like he had a huge smile on his face on the side I could see. I wondered if he had a similar one on the other side and what it might mean if he did. Nothing good, I thought.

We sat down, Father taking the chair with his back to the wall, and me sitting right beside him where I could watch.

"That guy from the alley is at the bar now," I whispered to Father. "He has a big scar on his face and looks like a Maleseet or Passamaquoddy, maybe a Micmac." Passamaquoddy Indians were from New Brunswick, but Maleseets could come from either side of the border. They were there long before Canada and the United States became countries, as were Micmacs who lived in Prince Edward Island, or "PI's" as we called them. All three had easy to recognize, long facial features.

Father turned to me. "Keep an eye on him, but don't stare. Scan the bar every minute or so, and nudge me with your elbow if you see him move."

Soon, a very large man with a huge beard walked into the room from the door to the right of the bar and headed directly toward us. There was a gold ring in his right ear lobe. He pulled up a chair.

"Good to see you again." Father extended his hand.

"Same here." Mike smiled, and they shook hands.

"This is my son, Charlie." Father told him. "It's ok to talk in front of him. He works with us in the business now and knows enough to keep his mouth shut. Right, Charlie?" Father asked.

"Right," I said, with no real enthusiasm. I kept scanning the room, keeping Feather Man in sight. Mike pulled out two cigars, offering one to Father who politely declined.

Mike and Father talked business. I didn't understand everything, but what I did figure out was this: Father would supply Mike with twenty cases of good whiskey and rum every week. Mike showed Father a brown envelope which Father looked at. I could see some ends of bills. Later, I learned they were hundreds.

"These will be yours on delivery to the Dam." Mike put the envelope back in his pocket. "I'll have a truck there every Thursday afternoon to pick up your delivery. It won't do not to show up."

"You have no idea how rough the lake can be," Father said. "Might have to wait a day."

"No, we won't wait. Plan to come down the day before if you think there might be a problem. Maybe you could store some there in case. You have to keep the schedule," Mike warned. "We won't take kindly to coming all the way up there and coming back empty handed. You're not the only supplier, you know. Mike looked toward the bar. Here's someone you need to meet," he said.

"Mike tells me you know a little about making 'shine," said a lady who was walking to the table. We stood. She had her arms hooked between two men on either side as if they were her escorts. The diamonds around her neck could have been glass, but she didn't seem to be the sort of woman who would wear paste jewelry. Bright red lips, red nails, and a tan dress that brought out the green of her eyes. From a distance the dress also brought out other attributes that I had a hard time not staring at. Low cut, fabric so thin I didn't know how it could even exist, left little to the imagination. She sat down in a rush of perfume that almost knocked me over. Father, Mike and I sat right after she did. As her escorts seated her, she extended her hand to Father.

"All the booze in Bangor goes through me." The men on each side stepped back, watching us closely.

"Fanny Mae Stillman," she introduced herself, "although I have to say there aren't too many still men around me, if you know what I mean," she smiled as a surprised Father took her hand. "You can call me Fanny," she smiled, first at him and then at me, tilting her head as if to get a better angle of my face. She dropped Father's hand and sat in Mike's chair.

"And who is this handsome young pup?" she asked, looking at me.

"This is my son, Charlie," Father said.

"My, Charlie's handsome! Takes after you, Caleb. Won't be long before he'll be coming to the Nighthawk for a little fun." The Nighthawk was Fanny's bar and brothel. She was looking right at me, and her eyes seemed to flash. "I have some young friends, about your age, who would love to meet you."

I began to feel a little flushed, warm in my face. When we talked about it later, Father explained that I was blushing, what that meant, and what Fanny meant. I learned a lot on that trip.

"The reason you are able to do business in Bangor is because I allow it." She looked at Mike while tossing her hair. He nodded his head just a little. "I have a temporary supply problem with increased interceptions of my speed boats coming into Penobscot Bay carrying my deliveries."

"The Coast Guard has been trying out some faster boats recently," Mike chimed in. He had taken the chair across from Father.

Fanny shot him a look as if she had expected him to be silent. Mike dropped his eyes and examined the table top. She turned to Father.

"Whether or not I'm able to solve my transportation problems, I still want you to supply me with weekly shipments." Fanny adjusted her hair, flicking up the back. I think that was for Father's benefit. "I expect on-time delivery each week. My businesses here count on it. For your own safety and the safety of your family, you need to understand this."

It looked like Father was having difficulty restraining himself. I don't think I'd ever heard anyone talk to him that way. Father just glared at her for a moment.

"You're clear about the arrangement," Father said, "but let me be clear with you." Fanny raised an eyebrow, and the smile faded from her face. Mike now stared into the nearly empty whiskey bottle in front of him.

"I keep my word, but I don't travel one way streets." Father's voice was calm, even, no emotion at all. Her response was not quick enough for him. "It's a simple matter, isn't it?"

"Of course," she said. "Business depends on the market, which I control. We don't want trouble, but we do know how to solve problems."

Fanny stood up. Father, Mike and I stood, too.

"I'll see that you get a bottle of my special reserve," said Father. Later I found out there was no special reserve; it was Father's sarcasm that I didn't pick up.

As Fanny walked from the table with a man on each arm, she turned her face briefly and winked at me. I was a little uncomfortable around her, and I didn't like her much. She wore way too much perfume. When she sat beside me, she looked like an old woman under a lot of makeup. There was something about her that I didn't trust, but I couldn't put my finger on it.

After Fanny left the table, Mike warned Father to watch out for her competition. A group from Boston had been muscling into the Bangor market recently.

"They're a rough bunch," said Mike. "One of our suppliers was found washed up in front of Fort Knox last month. He had been shot five times, the coroner reported. You do need to look over your shoulder, even way up there."

Fanny owned outright or partnered with all the bars in Bangor. As prohibition began, there were over sixty speakeasies throughout the city. Fanny also ran the girls from her Nighthawk house on the corner of State and Exchange.

Fanny's girls were young, pretty and desperate. Many had been lured to work in the textile mills in Lewiston where they slaved for pennies each week while their room, board and sundry purchases from the company store kept them in perpetual debt. Fanny would pay that debt, and the girls would work it off. Fanny must have thought it was a nice thing to do for someone in financial trouble, and her girls weren't really slaves, she must have told herself. They seemed to be willing participants in an illegal, but profitable business. Once they decided to go to work for Fanny, they lost any control of their lives they might have had, which wasn't much to start with. Like well treated slaves, their only freedom was a clandestine escape. But to where? Most couldn't go home again. None had skills beyond the ability to perform menial tasks. All were imprisoned in a lifestyle designed to please men.

"She takes real good care of them," Mike told us. "Every year she gets her girls all dressed up in the finest gowns and parades 'em right down Main Street past the grins of the men and the scowls of their wives."

Mike told the story of Fanny and her girls being part of the "Bangor's Finest" Fourth of July parade, strolling to the opening gates of the Bangor State Fair. The Woman's Christian Temperance League tolerated their presence at the tail end of the parade. That turned out to be the best place for them. It kept the crowds anticipating the spectacle of fancy ball room dresses, diamond necklaces and plunging necklines. According to Mike, the men watching along the route loved it. None of that made the lives of the women who worked for her any better.

Father and Mike shook hands again, and I followed Father out of the "Bearded Lady" into the alley and back to our truck.

....

Nothing we were doing seemed to be bad. We weren't hurting anyone, we told ourselves, just out to make a dollar like the next guy. We were manufacturers and Fanny was just a distributor for her customers. This was simply business, Father told me many times. Besides, we were sticking it to the government who had murdered my brothers, Will and Sam.

He also told me there were risks. More than one "secret" rum-running outfit in the state had been burned out, blown up, or ratted on. Fanny had muscle, and I wondered if she had arms long enough to reach our barn and hotel in the Village.

As we climbed into the truck, Father asked me if I had anything to report. Not having been to the city for a long time, I wouldn't have known what was out of place, so I just said, "No."

He looked at me a moment. "You'll remember the man sitting at the bar with the feather in his hat? I don't think these folks will ever visit us in the Village. But just in case, let me know if you ever see him again."

"Okay," wishing that I were back home catching bullfrogs and snakes so I could torment the village girls, feeling cool mud ooze between my toes. But not this. I wasn't ready for this. I didn't have a choice; Father expected me to help. Mother expected me to do as he asked. It was a simple equation, but I didn't like the sound of this business because of the risks. Somehow, it seemed really dangerous to become involved with Fanny and Mike. If the government hadn't taken them away from me, my brothers would be the ones helping our Father, looking out for me, and I could be a kid a little longer. I know that might sound selfish, but there is a huge difference between dodging bullets and mustard gas in the trenches and making Tanglefoot. Or so I thought.

Father believed that our home was out of their reach. We were isolated by whole townships of forest, lakes and rivers, too. Because

Father believed we were safe, I did, too. We were both wrong.

We drove out of Bangor, along Kenduskeag Stream. I was hoping for some supper soon. My stomach began talking to me about an hour before dinnertime, and it was screaming at me right now.

"We'll stay in Dover tonight if we're not followed," Father said. "Keep a watch for lights behind us. Use the mirror on the side of the door." I kept watch again, looking for anything moving behind us, lights or not. Once I thought I saw a big moose crossing the road just ahead after we got into East Corinth, but I wasn't really sure. In the mirror I saw what I thought was a pair of black wings closing in on us. I kept blinking my eyes, but the wings were still there coming closer and then falling back. I had heard stories about black wings before. The Norembegas believed their appearance presaged the death of a tribal leader. After what happened on the boat later on, I now think it was Ki'kwa'jenu following us home. I doubted that even strong winds sent by the spirit of Katahdin would have pushed him away.

We got to the Blethen House in Dover around eight. This was the half-way mark between Greenville and Bangor. The stage still stopped here, delivering merchants, loggers and sometimes sports from Bangor or the train station in town. Father got us a room, and we went downstairs to a lavish dining area for something to eat. Several large crystal chandeliers lit up round tables that were covered with white linen. It was a decent supper, fresh scrod from Bangor with just picked fiddleheads and freshly made biscuits. We ate with no conversation. I thought about the friends Fanny had who would like me. I didn't think I'd like them.

That night, I saw the same black wings in my dreams. Somehow, I was able to push them away with thoughts of a strong gust of wind. I didn't sleep well, and I awoke exhausted from my efforts of self-defense.

The next morning, we were off after a breakfast of bacon, eggs, steak and bean-hole beans. It wasn't long before we got to Greenville where we loaded more supplies, and then we were off to the Grant Farm where we had lunch. I didn't see any black wings the rest of the trip.

Besides Dan Call, the master distiller from Jack Daniels, there were ten men waiting for us at the Grant Farm for a truck ride to Chesuncook Dam and then a boat ride up the lake. These were river drivers who risked their lives every day floating logs from the river bank landings into the waiting booms. They made two dollars a day, and that was before taking out the charges for boots, socks, pick poles and Peaveys. When a hat cost two dollars and a pair of pants went for five, sometimes there wasn't much left in the season's last pay envelope, just as our flea-bitten passenger had said.

These migrant workers arrived at the Grant Farm the night before, after a steamer ride across Moosehead, followed by a truck ride the next ten miles to the farm. Some were Pollacks, a word we used to refer to Lithuanians, Latvians, Yugoslavs and Poles. It wasn't a bad word, not then. Occasionally there'd be a Canadian, a PI (Prince Edward Island), an Italian or a German. Sometimes a Russian. Many settled in the area and raised families. Some died on the rivers, lakes and woods trying to make a better life while making millions for the Company. When one died on the drive and if the body was found, there would be a burial in the Company's lot in Greenville. And when the remains were never found, there might be a little service in our church. The river drivers' spiked boots would be hung from a tree branch beside the rapid where they had drowned.

By that evening, all the river drivers were safe and sound in the new driving camps up the West Branch. The cargo of Moxie crates and all the supplies were stored in the barn. Dan Call, Uncle Amos and Father stayed up late designing and planning the operation. I overheard some talk about aging the product. I was glad to be back home. It took two baths to wash off the miles of road dust. Thoughts of Fanny's friends and dreams of those black wings stayed with me for more than a few days.

Chapter 3

The next morning after breakfast, Father put me to work.

"This morning," he told me, "you'll be with Uncle Amos in the barn. You're done with school now, and I need you to help out. I'll pay you every month."

"Okay," I said.

"You'll have to keep a sharp eye for anything or anyone unusual. Just be really sure you never talk about what we do or about our trip. You heard what Mike said about the Boston gang. We need to keep an eye out for them, just in case. Understand?"

"Okay," I said. "I won't say anything."

Last night, after I went to bed, Father and Uncle Amos unloaded the boat in the dark, tired as Father was from bouncing over the roads to Bangor and back. Although everyone here knew what we were up to, Father decided it would be best to unload that night in case someone wanted to help themselves to some of the cargo. He and Uncle Amos put the sacks of sugar, dried fruit and corn in the back room of the barn where the still was, and then they stacked up the cases of empty Moxie bottles beside them. The honey was kept in large kegs. The yeast was kept in an old pie safe.

It was easy for me to learn from my Uncle Amos. He had come with us to the village years ago. Although he had no children of his own, he was an uncle to all the village kids. He was clean shaven and well educated. Uncle Amos knew how to make the best 'shine in the state, and he taught me well. With Dan Call's help, our Tanglefoot was the best in the East.

The first still was a 55-gallon round copper tank that had a smaller tank soldered on the top. The 'shine meandered through copper coils, slowly dripping into a huge glass jug, once used for office water coolers. In one stove, Uncle Amos kept a small fire to cook the mash, and another wood stove heated water that circulated in a large copper tank beside it for washing out the bottles, one of the jobs assigned to me. I hated washing bottles. It took several days to get the Moxie smell off my hands, and although my nails had never been cleaner, my hands were raw and chapped from all the water and caustic soap. Mother gave me some cream to sooth the raw skin. That helped, but I thought the scent was a little too strong.

In the next month, Uncle Amos would set up several more stills in the large back room of the barn, a single-story addition built a decade ago to house teams of horses. Racks of drying Moxie bottles I had washed took over one entire wall. Three stills were on the opposite wall with all the smoke stacks going into one fieldstone chimney towering far above us.

Like a beacon, smoke was a serious problem with any still. Government agents could see exactly where a still was and would then bust up the operation. Because a forge was often in use in our barn, no one questioned the smoke coming from the barn's chimney. Maybe it was the smithy working. Who would know? Everyone in the village would, but none cared.

Using the bottling machine that Uncle Amos designed and built, our product was repacked in the original Moxie bottles and wooden crates. These were stacked by the back door. On delivery days, Uncle Amos and I would load the cases in the wagon and Duke would tug it all to the dock where we transferred the 'shine to the boat for its trip down the lake to Fanny's truck, waiting to take it all to Bangor.

After Father brought the finished cases of Tanglefoot, Blackbeard Rum and Sweet Feed 'Shine down the lake, sometimes at night, he then loaded the *Tethys* with the grains, yeast and sugars plus the cases of empty Moxie bottles that were brought from Bangor on the return trip. We needed something to put the Tanglefoot in, and these empty Moxie bottles were perfect. Costs were minimal. We would rake in more than Dr. Kilmer's Swamp Root Elixir earned for that charlatan, that's for sure. Advertised to cure kidney, liver and bladder problems, the elixir was twenty percent alcohol. Our Tanglefoot was 190 proof. We could run the boat on it.

If Father had to make a special night's run down the lake rum-running, it raised few questions in our little village. Folks seemed to know what was going on and minded their own business. Whenever there were large jobs around the farm, Father hired as many of the locals as he could. He paid them well, either in cash, store credit or Tanglefoot. Most took the store credit. Moonshining paid my family well and it also gave our isolated community a boost. There was no Temperance north of Dover, the Piscataquis County Seat. There was no law, either.

Dan Call got us set up the right way. His recipe consisted of rye, corn, prunes and apricots when we could get them and apples when we could not, raisins, yeast and sugar. These were dumped into a fifty-gallon oak barrel. After warm water was added to the two thirds mark, the barrel was kept warm to ferment for five or six days. The juice from this mash was strained, then poured into the copper cooking still. Several batches of fermented juice could be drawn from one barrel of mash.

After the juice was added, the copper pot was heated on a wood stove just shy of boiling. Condensing at the top of the still, the 190-proof alcohol dripped through a descending copper coil into another barrel, this one lower and filled with cold water. The end of the coil came out the bottom of the barrel. Where it exited the barrel, the hole around the tube was packed with strands of waxed hemp, keeping the cold water from leaking out.

We could get two to three gallons of clear moonshine from each batch. Some folks called it "White Lightning," but ours wasn't clear for long. Since the big money was in the amber color in standard whiskey, we colored it by adding a little lemon and orange syrup. Some 'shine was aged in oak barrels without the coloring. The oak wood added a nice brown tone to those batches. We called it *Tanglefoot*. When the first batch was in the bottles, Dan's work was finished. He went back down the lake with Father on the next trip.

My job was to keep the water cold in the condensing barrel, watch the mash to keep it from reaching the boiling point, and help Uncle Amos bottle it all up in Moxie bottles and cases. It seemed that I could never take a break, there was so much to do. It was hard work. We never had to worry about being raided by the Feds, as we lived too far away from everything, and the County Sheriff on Father's generous payroll would give us a heads-up if we needed to tear it all down and hide it away. That happened only once.

When they did raid us, the barn was clean, equipment was hidden in another barn, and we hid our stock in the pig pen and the privy. That was the only time we ever called our batch "crappy."

Chapter 4

The morning after my first Bangor trip with Father, I went out to the barn to see Uncle Amos. Always neatly dressed, he was wearing a leather apron that covered his red suspenders. The heavy boots he wore were good protection from a misplaced oxen or horse hoof. As our village blacksmith, he knew not to take chances with fussy critters. When I came through the door, it looked like he had just finished re-shoeing another horse.

"How ya doin', Charlie?" he asked. "Recovered from your traveling?" I walked over to the pile of Moxie crates where he was standing and took out an empty bottle.

"Sort of," I said. Then, Father walked into the barn. The bright sun was behind him, making him look like a black shadow with no face.

"About time you got up," Uncle Amos jibed at my Father.

"And I suppose you've been here since the crack of dawn?"

"Maybe not that early," Uncle Amos grinned at him. He was always grinning. I don't know how a sense of humor nailed Uncle Amos but completely missed Father. Uncle Amos and Father didn't even look much alike for brothers. Father was quite a bit shorter with a barrel chest, more like Mother's height. Uncle Amos was tall like me with the muscular arms of someone who pounded red hot steel all day. He was always having to duck his head as he passed through low doorways in the hotel.

"You give Charlie his marching orders yet?" Father wanted to know, standing there with his hands on his hips, as if asserting his authority with his voice, always the loudest in the room.

"Just about to when your ugly face darkened the barn door. Why don't you go do something useful and let me take care of this end?" Uncle Amos asked. Father must have thought better than to reply to Uncle Amos' comments. Sometimes these brothers could get into a fiery argument about nothing. Without a word, Father turned on his heel, marched out the door, most likely going back to the kitchen for another cup of Mother's coffee and a freshly baked corn muffin.

"Your father seems to have been picking his teeth with a rusty nail again. Here, Charlie, help me fill the still," Uncle Amos said, handing me two pails. I smiled at his comment as I grabbed the buckets and walked over to the hand pump in the front corner of the barn. Father had dug a well; having the pump inside made it easier to take care of the animals. The steel handle had become smooth and free of paint after years of use. As the pump pulled up water from the well below, the handle's squeal echoed through the barn. The animals that lived there were used to it and didn't respond to that ear-piercing noise. I wondered why Uncle Amos never greased it.

I pumped away, filling buckets, emptying buckets, and doing it all over again until the bottom of the boiling tank was covered with several inches of water.

Uncle Amos lit a small fire with one of the wooden matches he kept under his hat. He measured the corn, sugar and yeast, dumping it all in the tank. When I asked him why he kept matches under his hat, he said, "Your grandfather taught me that trick. Matches keep dry there, and you never know when you might need one."

This wasn't the first batch Uncle Amos had made this spring, but it was one of his best, thanks to Dan Call. In large barrels stored in the back of the barn was some of the best Tanglefoot Moonshine ever made. It even had the brownish tint of Canadian whiskey, I later learned. Soon, the contents of those oak barrels would be ready to sell to customers who would tangle up their feet after just a few sips.

My next chore was filling the empty Moxie bottles from four barrels along the opposite wall. Placed on their side in a special rack about three feet off the ground, each had a little spigot making it easy to transfer the liquor to the bottles resting on a little shelf in front of each. The spigot was hammered in place and never leaked.

"Be careful you don't spill anything," Uncle Amos warned. "Every drop is worth a nickel." I remember looking at him, wondering if he was going to instruct me on how to turn the spigot on and off. I did know a few things, and I knew this job was the most boring one of all.

"I'll be careful," I told him, biting my tongue. I've had to do that a lot with both my Father and Uncle. Even though Uncle Amos was more forgiving, he did have limits.

Although it bored me to tears, filling bottles was the easy part. The hard part was inserting the corks. Darned things would break if I weren't careful about how I positioned the bottle in the corking machine Uncle Amos cobbled together. Placing the cork in the little holder first, I then pulled the handle down, and the cork slid into the bottle nice and tight. How hard and fast I pulled the handle determined whether or not the cork would break in the process. The bottles went back into the cases, and by noon the next batch was cooking away. The barrels I didn't draw from would be emptied over the next two weeks into more bottles with a Moxie label.

Most moonshiners kept their stills outside in the weather, often with a lean-to shielding the setup from the rain, but those rarely made the quality 'shine we did. Besides, Uncle Amos was using a recipe directly from the Jack Daniels distillery using dried fruit that gave the moonshine a distinct flavor and traditional color.

I helped Uncle Amos and Father load the *Tethys* with the crates of Moxie that wasn't Moxie. There were twenty wooden crates of bottles that we covered with a dark green canvas always kept on board.

Father took the boat down the lake to make the delivery. A few passengers were aboard, river drivers who had finished their contracts. As I walked to the lower village on an errand for Mother, I saw the *Tethys* scoot by on her way to the Dam, and I wished I was on it. After he dropped off any passengers and supplies at the Cuxabexis Depot across the lake on his return trip, Father would be home by supper with more sugar, corn, yeast, empty Moxie bottles, and a tan envelope full of more money than we had ever seen. I'd save my first pay for the bike I had seen in the Bangor Mercantile. Maybe that sixteen gauge Winchester shotgun was within reach, too. Father kept talking about the potato farm in Aroostook County he wanted to buy.

That night, I had the scariest dream. I looked out at the barn and could see it was on fire. Flames shot out the little windows along the front, and smoke was coming from under the edge of the roof. I could hear someone screaming from inside, and then silence. I woke up in a sweat. I didn't know who or what was screaming. That bothered me more than the image of the barn in flames.

Chapter 5

After lunch, Mother asked me to go to Hiram's to get some eggs. Our hens were young, and they hadn't started laying yet.

"Tell him we need two dozen today and the day after tomorrow, too. We have company due when your Father gets back from the Dam, and I forgot to put eggs on the grocery list I gave to Father." Mother shooed me out the door with two empty egg boxes, and I walked the mile to the lower village to find Hi.

Hiram Francis often worked for my father. He did odd jobs that Father didn't have time for and I hadn't been old enough to help with, like climbing up on the thirty-foot scaffold and shingling the four-story barn roof.

He was a member of a Micmac tribe in Nova Scotia. Preferring the company of his chickens over humans, Hiram lived alone in a little log cabin he built from the fir and spruce trees on his lot. His cabin had a deep cellar hole, a natural refrigerator and excellent root cellar for potatoes, turnips, apples, beets and onions. Sometimes he had pigs and a goat in a little shed out back. Tall pines grew in back of the camp. Some were over seventy-five feet tall. I know that because I had helped Father cut down some just like them for sawing boards at our mill by the barn. From each tree, I helped measure five sixteen-foot logs, marking where to make the cut and being careful to add a few inches to each log for trim.

Hiram was throwing out some corn for his flock of Barred Rocks when he heard my footsteps coming up the wooded path to his camp. It wasn't often he had a social visitor. Most came on business and respected his privacy. On occasion, the hotel would need extra eggs, and from the empty egg cartons he could see me carrying under my arm, it was obvious that's what my visit was about.

Hiram came here to work for the Company in the summers. After a few seasons of river driving, Hi decided to build this small cabin at the south end of the village. He knew a lot about Indian spirits and their stories. I heard Mother say that Hiram was a well-respected shaman.

I loved to hear his stories. The scariest one was about a spirit bird with long, black wings and a sharp beak meant for ripping apart flesh. He called it the Nighthawk, and I remembered that was also the name of Fanny's place. I thought I saw black wings chasing me and Father on our Bangor trip, but that was probably just a suggestion in my young mind from hearing his stories. Or maybe it was from learning that Fanny had a business with the same name.

"Hello, Charlie," he said, without looking. He could tell by my gait and light step just who it was. His senses were that sharp. No other youngster would dare come up here, but I wasn't afraid of Hi regardless of all the critter skulls nailed to trees along the path to his cabin.

"Mornin', Hi," I said. "Mother would like some eggs if you have any to spare." Under my arm I carried two empty egg cartons.

"She can have two dozen," he told me. "They're fresh the last two days. Those hens have been laying like crazy."

Hiram had a dozen laying hens that seemed pretty amazing. He might sell three or four dozen eggs in a day. A hen lays one egg in a day, sometimes in two days. They never could have laid enough eggs to supply the demand, but somehow Hiram always had plenty. I solved the puzzle of the super chickens when I saw a thousand egg crate loaded in Father's boat, bound for Hiram's. He ordered eggs from Bangor and kept that large egg crate in the hen house, pretending to bring up "fresh eggs" from the chicken coop when an egg customer like me appeared at his cabin.

"She'd like that," I said. "She said to ask if she could have two dozen more in a couple of days. More woodsmen on their way, I guess." And after handing him the fifty cents, he filled the two cartons.

"I'll save some for her," he said.

But I didn't just leave. I had to ask about what I thought I had seen on the trip back from Bangor. Hiram would know what it was.

"Hi, would you tell me the story about the Nighthawk again?" I asked. Hiram studied me for a moment.

"Why do you ask, Charlie?"

"On our trip back from Bangor, I thought I saw something flying behind us. It was bigger than an owl or a raven. And I've had some bad dreams about black wings, too."

"Ki'kwa'jenu is his real name. He is a spirit whose power was becoming weaker by the day. To become strong again, Ki'kwa'jenu had to find and devour one with power, power that was used for bad things," Hiram began. "He used his large black wings to take his quarry back to his nest by Pamola on the Big Hill, our Katahdin. After he devoured his prey, Ki'kwa'jenu was strong again."

When Hi finished his story, I was pretty sure I had seen Ki'kwa'jenu on that trip, and I wondered if I were Ki'kwa'jenu's prey. I didn't think I had any power that Ki'kwa'jenu would want. I was just a kid. I had to ask him.

"If I've seen the wings of Ki'kwa'jenu, does it mean that I have something he wants?"

"There are many ways that shamans learn they have abilities beyond the rest of us. Being followed by Ki'kwa'jenu is one, but thinking you've seen him could be just a reminder that death is always following us. Was your time in Bangor challenging at all?"

I didn't know what to tell Hi. Father didn't want me to talk about business, and what we did in Bangor was supposed to be kept quiet even though the entire village, including Hiram, knew what the family business was.

"Bangor is a very different place. I was a little afraid, especially when I thought those black wings were following us on the way to Dover that night. I felt they were coming for me."

"And you weren't able to call up the winds to help, were you?" I didn't know what to say. How could Hiram have learned my deepest secret? I'd never told anyone.

"What do you mean?" I asked, pretending not to know what he was talking about. The winter before, I was ice fishing off the village cove. I walked out to check the flag that had flipped up. When I pulled up the line, a huge salmon appeared at the other end. As soon as the giant fish hit the ice, it spit out the hook and wiggled itself back down the hole he had just come out of. I was furious. Just as I was looking for something to throw at the hole in the ice, strong winds came up out of a clear sky, blowing me back to shore. When I calmed down, the winds stopped. Or was it the other way around? Standing on the shore, staring at the ice hole I had just been blown away from, I became angry once again, thinking about that nice salmon I wasn't going to be eating for supper. And again, the wind rose. I calmed myself down, and so did the wind.

"Charlie, some people have an aura about them that only a few others can see. I can see a glow surrounding you. It has a meaning."

"What does it mean?" I asked. I'd never heard anything like it, but of anyone here, Hi would know.

"It means that you can do some things that no one else can do. In your case, when you're angry, you can summon the winds. Wasn't that what you were testing out after the wind blew you to the shore?" Hi looked at me, eyebrows raised a little, anticipating my response. It was creepy how he could have known.

"Charlie, I was at Fred's place on the cove when that happened. I saw the wind push you across the ice to shore."

"But why couldn't I bring the winds to chase away the black wings that were following us on the way home from Bangor?"

"You said you were afraid then, right?" Hiram said.

I had a moment of clarity. "Then that's the difference. I was angry about losing the salmon. I was afraid when I saw the black wings."

"That would be my guess, too. Understanding power is different for each young shaman. There's no easy answer. Sometimes it takes years to learn how to control those powers, but it can be done. It's up to you to focus and be more aware when you're angry or afraid."

"I hope it's soon," I said. "It's really confusing sometimes." I had had enough of probing how I was feeling. "Can we talk more about this later on?"

"Sure, Charlie, whenever you want."

Changing the subject, I asked, "Will you be coming back to work at the hotel?" Hiram had been doing odd jobs for us. He was good on the barn roof, a place Father never climbed up to. I think Father was afraid of heights but would never admit it.

Hiram thought about that question a minute. Working for Father wasn't easy; he could be pretty demanding. The last time he hired Hiram, the job was to set out fence for Father's critters. Father made Hi reset half the posts. They were leaning a little too much one way or the other. I remember they all looked just fine to me. After Hi reset the posts, Father paid him for his extra time, and I know Hiram appreciated that. Father knew the value of time here, even though it did pass slowly in the village summers.

My father wasn't an easy man to do business with. One season Hi collected scrap iron from the remains of old logging camps, old broken stoves and such, rusty farm equipment from the fields on the island, piled it high on a log raft he made, and polled it all the way to the hotel to sell it. Hiram tied the raft up to the shore in front of the hotel and sought out Father.

"I've got that iron all collected," I remember hearing him tell Father, who was relaxing on the front porch reading last month's paper.

"What iron?" Father swatted away some deer flies.

"The iron you said you'd pay me for if I collected it and rafted it to the cove," Hi stated.

"I never said I would pay you for it Hi, but I did say I'd help you sell it," Father told him. Father was right. I was there when they had that conversation, and I don't know why Hiram remembered it the way he did. Maybe Hi really needed money and his imagination got the best of him, seeing money where there really wasn't any. Sometimes I think disagreements like this was the reason Hi preferred to live alone, hermit-like in an isolated place.

Hiram then said a few things he shouldn't have, and Father just turned his back and walked to where I was watching by the pig sty, pretending to fix the gate. Hi stormed back to the shore and untied the raft. He split apart the logs, letting the iron fall to the bottom of the lake right beside Father's float. There was a pile of it, over two tons. Father wasn't too happy with Hiram, but in Hiram's mind they were even enough. When the water drops to its lowest level in the fall after the rear of the drive comes through, that pile is right in Father's face every time he gets into his boat. Father has never said a word about it, and he's never tried to move it.

I waited a long time for Hi's answer.

"If your father asks, I'd be willin'," he said. "Now you run along home, hear?"

"Yes, sir," I replied.

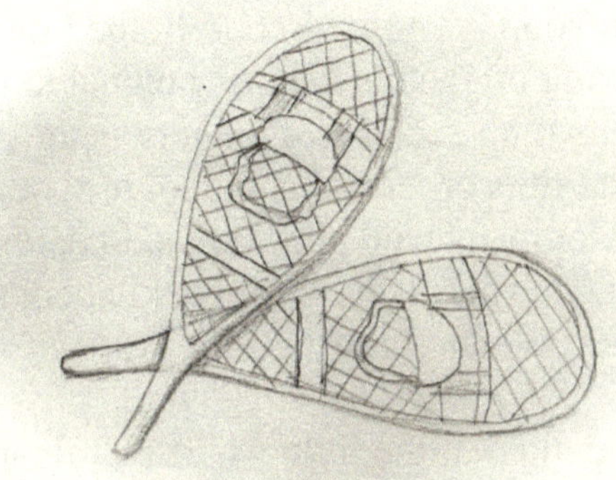

Chapter 6

"Get your coat," father shouted upstairs to me, "and meet me at the boat. We're going right now. Hurry up." I was needed to help with loading the cargo on this last trip of the season, now the end of November. There was no one else to help, as Uncle Amos had gone down river to secure more supplies for making Tanglefoot through the winter. We would eat a late lunch at the Boom House at the Dam. Earlier that morning, I finished loading the cases of Moxie that wasn't Moxie in the *Tethys*. I ran upstairs to get some warmer clothes on.

I grabbed my things and headed to the dock where Father had already started up the *Tethys*. There was smoky exhaust gurgling in a cloud of steam from the stern as her engine warmed up. My first chore was pumping out the bilge. We had a hand pump that emptied out the water which had been leaking in ever since we hit a deadhead on one recent trip to the Depot. I cast off, hopped in, and we were under way. Two hours later, we tied up to the Company pier at the Dam and walked over to the dining hall. The water was lower than normal since pulp wood had been flushed down the river to the mills. It was either a twenty-foot climb up a ladder to the top of the pier or a walk across a wet and slippery gang plank from the float to shore. We took the gang plank.

"Hey, Caleb," the bull-cook hollered as we came up the steps, "did you bring me my special order?" he asked as Father led us through the door to the dining area.

"Right here," and Father handed him a brown paper bag with a bottle of Tanglefoot inside.

"My aching joints will really appreciate this," he said, handing

Father ten dollars. "Have a seat, and I'll get you two some lunch. It's cold out today. Storm's comin' in soon." The bull-cook limped away to get our meal. He had been working on the diversionary tunnel to the new power station when he got blown up because of a faulty detonator on some dynamite. His left eye and the corner of his mouth drooped a little, and he had a game leg. The Company paid him well and kept him happy. His job as a bull-cook meant he was in charge of the kitchen, the ordering of food, firewood for the stove and directing the work of the cookee, the bull-cook's assistant.

Fanny's crew was already parked at the little wharf that floated beside the tall pier where we had tied up. Walking back and forth over a gang plank to shore, two men were busy unloading the crates of Moxie bottles. Then they got in their truck and waited near the cargo piled on shore beside the gang plank. I looked away from the window to dig into the steaming bowl of beef stew the cookee had brought over. I didn't realize how hungry I was. The biscuits were still fresh and warm, and I felt better right away.

While I was eating, I glanced out the window again, and this time I thought I saw a thin man walk to the float carrying a small leather satchel, one you'd carry tools in. Father had finished eating and was busy with the paper. This was not a good time to bother him with what I thought I saw since I just wasn't sure to begin with. Soon, the maybe Feather Man walked back to one of the already loaded trucks, hopped in on the passenger side, and the truck drove away.

"What are you staring at so intently?" Father asked.

"I thought I saw the guy from the bar leaving the pier." I said.

"What guy? Point him out," Father directed.

"I don't see him now," I said. "He was the one with the scars on his cheeks. He might have left in that truck." Father watched a truck drive away from where I pointed for a minute, then sat back down to finish his pie and read his paper.

We thanked the bull-cook for a nice lunch, and we walked back to the boat.

"Charlie," Father said, "I want you to load and secure the cargo in the *Tethys*. Be sure that it's centered. Take two of those men with you, and choose ones who can speak English, but don't let the rest of the men on the boat until all the dunnage is loaded first, understand?"

"Yes, sir," I said.

"Uncle Amos should be arriving soon from down river. He can help, too, if he ever gets here." I think I understood why Uncle Amos took his time coming back whenever he got the chance to get away. There was a lot of cargo to load.

Father walked to a little cabin to arrange storage space for our winter's production, and I went back to the *Tethys* to load the cargo with two of the strongest looking immigrants. After we passed the language barriers, I chose two to help me. Both looked to be as strong as Thunder and Lightning. One of them whistled tunes the whole time. Uncle Amos showed up just as we finished loading the last hundred-pound keg of horseshoes. He always timed things well. I don't like to think about how our fates would be different had Uncle Amos missed the boat that night.

Chapter 7

Just as the sun began to drop behind Caucmagomic Mountain, the *Tethys* was ready to take the woodsmen and cargo up Chesuncook Lake to the Company's Depot, kitchen and lodging house. Late that November afternoon, Father backed the *Tethys* away from the Company pier at the Dam. On a nicer day, the sun would have been shining still on the mile-high summit of Mt. Katahdin when we rounded Weymouth Point, the halfway mark. On this cloudy afternoon there was sun, but there was no wind, and there was no warmth. Chesuncook Lake had begun to freeze. You could see it happening. The swell from the boat's bow undulated just enough to see the paper-thin sheets of icy glaze beginning to form as Father piloted the *Tethys* to the Cuxabexis Depot.

At fifty-two feet, the *Tethys* carried thirty-five passengers and their gear that late Fall afternoon. She had been a Downeast shrimper when the Bangor & Aroostook Railroad bought her. The railroad company renamed her after the Greek Mother of the River Gods.

Her journey from Bangor began on the B&A's thirty-mile track to Guilford. From there, nestled in her protective cradle, the *Tethys*, hauled by a team of sixty oxen over freshly iced roads, went to Greenville. I can only imagine the sight of thirty pair of those huge beasts, heavy yellow birch oxbows over their shoulders, ice cleat shoes on their cloven hooves, their tenders trudging the next thirty miles to Moosehead Lake beside them, urging them to pull harder.

She had ferried passengers from the B&A depot at Rockwood and Greenville to their fancy hotel at Mt. Kineo for a few years before Henry Capin bought her for his "modern hostelry" on Moosehead's Deer Island. She was then sold to The Company, put back on her protective cradle and dragged to Canada Falls where she was discovered to be too big for the shallow flowage there. Cradled once more, she was skidded over land to Northeast Carry to tow on Moosehead, and once more overland from Lily Bay to Chesuncook Dam to tow more wood there. The Company moved her back over land once more to Moosehead. No wonder Father called her "the land boat." When Father needed to replace his aging, leaking steamer with something larger and newer so he could continue ferrying passengers and cargo up Chesuncook Lake for his contract with the Company, he found the *Tethys* was a good boat and at a good price.

Getting the *Tethys* back from Moosehead to her new berth at Chesuncook Dam was nearly as slow as the oxen power that helped get her to Moosehead in the first place. She was taken out at Lily Bay on her cradle to be hauled to the Dam by three Holt tractors chained together in a line. Paying by the hour and not the job was Father's mistake. The tractors kept breaking down and towing chains kept snapping. It took nearly fourteen hours to travel the twenty-five miles to Chesuncook Dam. "You don't want to know the cost," he told me once.

There were more than two tons of supplies for the five logging camps at the head of Chesuncook Lake on the *Tethys* this November afternoon. These supplies would not last until spring break-up six months away when the crews would be let go after the winter pulpwood quotas had been met, but they would last long enough until a re-stocking trip in January. The lake ice would be thick then, and the haul roads would be smoothed out with frozen, packed snow. We loaded logging chains, cross-cut saw blades, even steel for the blacksmith, shoes both for seventy or so residents who depended on the tiny village store and for the three hundred horses that hauled the cord wood from the cut to the landing at some water's edge. This was her last trip for the season, just before ice-up. There would be no boat traffic on Chesuncook Lake for at least another month when the ice might be safe enough to travel over by sleigh.

Also on board were three thirty-gallon barrels of gasoline, four barrels of kerosene and two cases of dynamite for the occasional stubborn stump or boulder. And of course, twenty cases of empty Moxie bottles, grains, dried fruit and cakes of yeast.

The kerosene was for the lanterns. It gets dark by 4:30 through the end of December, and light was needed well before 4 AM when the men began their day. Kerosene lamps and replacement chimneys were also in the *Tethys'* cargo. I helped load figs of tobacco, kegs of ax heads (they made their own handles at the camps), peaveys, pick poles, oars, paddles, clothing, a few barrels of potatoes grown just twenty miles away at the Grant Farm, and several decks of cards to help the men pass the time.

There was a keg or two of cut nails, barrels of long spikes, saw blades, coils of heavy hemp rope, flour, and, of course, sacks and sacks of beans, the woodsman's staple. Four times a day the men ate beans and then more beans after that. Grown at the Company's farms, beans were easy to store and haul about, and easy to bake in the cast iron Bangor Clarion wood cook stove.

Aboard were new wood cutters, mostly immigrants and Indians for the five camps the Company had constructed the month before. We were thirty-four in all.

Across from Big Mouser Island, I would be able to see the flat top of Big Spencer Mountain and the little bump on top of Lobster Mountain to the northeast had it not been for the slate grey lowering clouds drifting in. The thin film of ice forming on Chesuncook's surface could disappear with a light wind.

Chapter 8

One of our passengers was Louis Maki. Two years earlier, when he was just 18, Louis was traveling to Boston looking for work when he saw a poster in the Union Street Oyster House looking for woodsmen. He signed on to work for the Company, but not as a wood cutter. Always wearing an engineer's cap, Louis was the telephone line scout and repairman for the bare wire telephone network between the Village, camps and Grant Farm. He was returning home the long way around with a free boat ride back up the lake.

Louis had been walking for three weeks, checking the phone wire from Chesuncook Village, past Deer Pond Camps, past Ragged Stream and at last to the Grant Farm, where they ended at the switchboard's home. Checking the line meant raising sagging wires off the ground, replacing broken eight-foot poles, and splicing broken wire. He was looking forward to being back to his camp, sleeping in a real bed, and having a venison feed from the doe he had been watching that summer as she grazed in the field by Graveyard Point.

"Hey, Louis," Father greeted him with a firm handshake. "Good to have you aboard." Louis wasn't his usual neat self after hanging out in the woods with the moose and bears. He hated bears.

Uncle Amos told several stories about bears and Louis. Once, Louis was boiling sap in a little shanty on the shores of Caribou Lake. His sugar house was on a steep hillside. Its roof was pretty flat, coming out straight from the bank. The back wall was a bank of dirt. Louis had seen signs of bear when collecting sap, and he took no chances of the critter getting into his sugar house. While inside, Louis nailed a cross cut saw blade over the door and a couple of boards across the windows at each side.

Mr. Bear smelled something sweet, and being super hungry after a long winter's nap, sniffed about the roof of the sugar house. Walking out on the flat roof where he could really smell the sweet steam from the evaporator, the bear fell through.

Louis was now trapped inside the sugarhouse with the bear, boards across the windows and a saw blade across the door. He crawled up through the large hole in the roof the bear fell through, broke down his own door to let the beast out, and ran like hell.

"Hard trip?" Father asked. "You look beat."

"Damn insulators weren't no good," he complained. "Had to replace half the ones I put up last time. Then twice, moose tangled up their Christly horns and pulled a half dozen poles down each time. Too damned much work for what they pay." Then in a quieter voice, "Maybe I should be making 'shine with you and Amos instead."

Father looked sorry he had asked. "Louis, without you, there'd be no phone," and he smiled a bit. "Take the wheel, will you? I need to check on the engine, if you know what I mean."

"You're going to try that old ruse again? These guys look pretty tough, if you ask me. If they figure it out, you'll be swimmin' with the salmon."

"Damned right I'm going to do it. It's cold, I want a drink, and I don't have one handy. You?"

He didn't. Just because he was a rum runner, Father didn't always have a bottle of Tanglefoot within reach. Louis knew better than to push Father any more. A good friend should know when to stop, and Louis did.

After the *Tethys* passed Weymouth Point, her Brennan De Luxe Six quit. This 150- horsepower gasoline engine, advertised as "reliable since 1898," was made in Syracuse. There was "a Brennan Motor for every possible use," according to the advertisements. Her engine suddenly quitting made her passengers nervous, but not me, Father or Louis. Father was the one who had just closed the leaky fuel valve before going back to the helm.

After the *Tethy's* engine quit from fuel starvation, Father returned to her engine room, turning the air blue with curses. He knew he had to put on a good show, or this ploy wouldn't work. Everyone could hear him swearing and banging around as we drifted through the forming ice sheet. That was good; the annoyance and ire seemed real.

Louis turned to the concerned men now gathering around the

wheel house. "Captain King is a little out of sorts, as you can hear. A few swigs of whiskey will sooth his nerves, helping him focus on fixing whatever's wrong down there." The men just looked at each other.

"Does anyone have any?" Several flasks were immediately presented. Louis brought the largest one below. Behind the closed engine room door, Father and Louis drained it.

Father stopped cursing and clanging about as he turned the leaky fuel cock back on. The Brennan coughed to life, and we were quickly under way again. I'd seen him work this ploy more than once, but on this trip, something much warmer than whiskey waited for us.

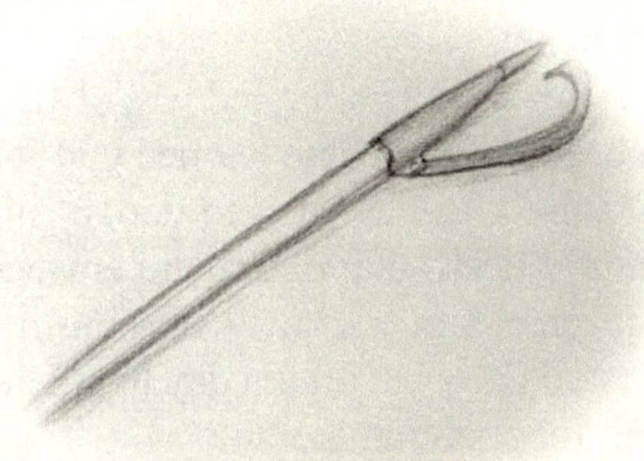

Chapter 9

On board were two boys about my age. They were huddled under a blanket on a side bench. Tommy and William Bridge were brothers who had shipped from Liverpool to Boston on a steamer, paying for their passage as cabin boys. It didn't take long after they saw the advertising flyers in the bars, the flophouses and the Union Street Oyster House for them to jump ship and make their X on the contract at the Company's Tremont Street office in Boston, indicating no next of kin like many migrants who came to work in the Maine woods. They handed their tickets to another steamer captain, and sailed up the Maine coast to Bangor, just one of several stops to the middle of nowhere. It must have seemed that way to those young boys, at least, as the urban settings they were traveling through became smaller and smaller, then disappeared entirely. "Cord Cutters Wanted," the flyer had said. "Top Wages Paid" was what caught their eye. They didn't know about the beans, the fleas, the lice, sleeping on old mattresses beside twenty other men in the same long room no cleaner than the horse hovel next door. They didn't know what was ahead of them at Cuxabexis Narrows, just a mile before their destination.

Jeb Flanders was with us. Father knew Jeb well. He didn't put up with any nonsense, and they saw eye to eye on most things. Jeb was the dam tender at Ripogenus and was hitching a ride up the lake to make it to his warm winter camp in the village. He had been pretty busy managing the water flow, flushing the wood down to the Millinocket mills.

He often had the village school teacher board with him and was really looking forward to seeing this new one who had arrived two months ago. I'd seen her; she wasn't too hard to look at. When I first saw her climb aboard the *Tethys* at the Company's pier, I wished I could go back to school to have her as my teacher.

One day Jeb shot Pete Petrorvich's dog. That hound was always coming around and killing a chicken or two. When Pete learned that Jeb had killed his dog, both Jeb and the school teacher had to dodge rifle bullets while cowering inside the camp. I heard that one round crashed through the closet door where the teacher hid, narrowly missing her shoulder. The sheriff came in and arrested Pete, but after a day in jail, he let him go and came back to arrest Jeb for shooting the dog.

We could see the long spine of ledges extending from the southern-most tip of Gero Island nearly two miles down the lake. In some places the ledge disappears into the dark water only to rise above the surface several times like a serpent's back. When the lake is full, the ledges can't be seen, but this late afternoon with a drained-down lake due to the season's log drives, the spine couldn't be missed. On one side of the spine was the main channel of Chesuncook. On our side was the outflow of Moose Pond, drowned out when Ripogenus Dam was built a few years earlier. Father pointed the *Tethys* away from the ledge spine on the left and toward the entrance to Moose Pond on the right. Clouds had lowered more, now hiding the top half of Sourbungee Mountain. If Sourbungee couldn't be seen from the Village, it meant the weather was about to change.

We came closer to the gap between Gero Island and the mainland, a passage considerably narrowed by the low water. Father throttled down in case he had to avoid a deadhead or floating pulp log that had escaped from one of the season's booms. The channel lay between steep clay banks and bleached bones of flooded out fir and spruce that littered the shore. Stumps of the giant pines stuck out of the water here and there, marking the passage like silent witnesses to the deforestation by Company cutters. Most of these giant stumps, sun bleached, were coated with a fine silt at the high-water line, remnants of the rich loamy soil their root systems had kept in place for centuries, soil that was soon to clog the channels of all the rivers downstream.

Chapter 10

Father ran the *Tethys* at slow speed so I could search for stumps and deadheads while I draped myself over the bow. A deadhead was a log floating vertically just under or just above the water's surface. Sometimes deadheads were stuck in the mud, making it more likely the log would crash through the hull. Uncle Amos was on the other side of the bow, watching with me. Huge piles of dri-ki, old stumps and bleached out logs were on both sides of the channel. When I looked up, I could make out the faint lights of the Depot about a mile ahead. It was starting to get dark, and it was so cold my teeth were chattering. I wasn't liking this job much. I could barely wiggle my fingers inside my gloves, and I don't think I could have seen a deadhead if one was lurking right in front of us.

"Get down in the engine room and check the gas," Father ordered, his voice booming to the bow over the engine noise. I jumped at the chance to warm up. The engine room was always hot. I made my way along the narrow gunnel as I held on to the canopy's supporting posts. It wasn't easy to squeeze by some of the crates tied down to the narrow pathway. I dropped into the cargo area between two of the men who had helped me with loading at the Dam. After stepping around the crowd on the rear deck, I got to the engine room. I found the front and rear fuel tanks empty. We were running on the smaller side tanks, both nearly full. On the far side of the engine, I noticed a black box. I had never seen it before. It was easy to miss it in that darker corner. Tucked away below the fan belt pulley, two wires connected it to the battery with little clips. I wanted to ask Father about it, but he was concentrating on navigation, and in no mood to hear any such question from me. Still, I tried.

"What's the box for on the engine?" I asked after I left the warmth of the engine room. I could barely get a word in between his commands. "Is it something new?"

"That's the control relay for the searchlight," he replied, thinking about something quite different, I later learned. Sometimes, Father seemed incapable of having more than one thing on his mind at a time; he could be so clearly focused. At this moment, it was the searchlight and what was wrong with it, not a mysterious black box below the fan pulley.

"Charlie, take the wheel," he shouted to me. The heat from the engine room had already left my body. The breeze from our forward motion seemed to bring the temperature down; the men looked really cold, some wrapped in blankets, many of them were shivering. I wondered how, if they were cold now, they would survive cutting wood this winter when twenty below was a warm day.

"That darn search light won't come on. Something's wrong with the wiring," he declared. I was about to tell him again what I had seen on the engine, but Father was on a mission and had no time to hear what I said; we'd need that search light to see the stumps as we approached the Depot.

"Okay," I said, and I came to the helm where Father held the wheel until I could grab it.

"Keep her heading straight for the Depot lights in the distance," he told me. "We can't afford to hit another deadhead. The boat's still leaking from the last one, and hitting one of those stumps would sink us."

"Okay. It took me a while to pump her out last time."

"Keep the boat straight for those lights and we'll be fine, understand?"

"Okay," I could see the lights of the Depot. They looked like feeble stars shivering through the trees that stood tall along the far ridge. It wouldn't be too hard to steer for it. Some of the men looked at me, probably wondering if I was old enough to steer the boat. What they didn't know was that I had been steering since I was ten.

Some migrant workers stood shoulder to shoulder, stuffed between crates of cargo like sardines in a can. All the benches were occupied. Like a game of musical chairs, passengers would move from a seat on a duffle bag, a crate of equipment, the benches along the gunwales, to standing in the middle along a line of canopy support posts. A few found their way near the bow, navigating the crates tied down along the narrow gunwales, but the cold late November air of the *Thethy's* forward motion soon drove them back to the sheltered lee behind the wheelhouse.

I had tried to talk with some of them, but many didn't speak much English. Some were experts at using a crosscut saw, hooking up a horse, and all were used to hard labor by the looks of them. They didn't need much English to do their jobs.

I saw several passengers filling their pipes and rolling their smokes from little pouches they carried. They'd share a match or get a light from someone's cigar. Striking their matches on anything rough enough, brass zippers, iron braces supporting the gunwales or suspender clips, sent sparks flying about.

Beside the helm, the engine room door was barely large enough to squeeze through. There was a small window through which the engine could be seen without opening the door itself. On the other side and down two steps, the Brennan was chugging away. All around it were small storage bins for spare parts like a water pump, fan belts, old blue Maxwell House coffee cans full of nuts, bolts, washers, and the stray small parts like cotter pins and grease fittings, carburetor parts and small springs. Father kept all parts, used or broken, just in case.

The engine fuel on the *Tethys* was kept in four separate tanks: one in the bow, one in the stern, and one to each side. Each tank held a little over fifty gallons of gasoline. Depending on the load and head winds, she had a range of six round trips before having to refuel. Father would switch tanks by opening and closing the fuel cocks leading from the tanks to the engine's carburetor through a main fuel manifold. Four lines, one from each tank, connected to that manifold, and a single line fed the engine's carburetor with its own main shut off. This arrangement made it easier to work on the engine. The main shut off is the one he always used when caging drinks.

The gasoline fed the engine by gravity; there was no complicated fuel pump to maintain. Unless the fittings around the fuel cocks were super tight, gasoline would seep out and enter the bilge, a watery, sludgy stinking mess of old engine oil, grease and gasoline, sloshing around the bottom most part of the hull. I learned that vibration from a nicked prop could loosen nuts, screws and fuel line connections like old amalgam fillings. If the fuel lines were not checked regularly, drips of gasoline into the bilge often went unnoticed. When small drops of fresh gas from the engine compartment combined with the fuel rich bilge, we were a bomb surrounded by the sides of a boat. The *Tethys* didn't need the barrels of gasoline and kerosene on her fantail to become a floating fireball.

"Charlie, head to the bow and be on the lookout for deadheads. Remember, this is where we hit one last time." Father took over the wheel and sent me to hang over the bow. He was being cautious and had throttled back even more. I think he knew he'd have to tinker with or even replace the brass propeller after the *Tethys* was hauled out for the winter and nestled safely in her cradle in a few days, and then there was that pesky fuel leak that needed fixing.

In the very slight current of Moose Pond Stream just beneath us, the forming ice had disappeared for a few yards only to re-form as we entered the dead calm water of Moose Pond itself.

Chapter 11

We motored on towards the Depot, Father steering while Uncle Amos and I kept watch for deadheads off the bow. Once in a while, I glanced back to the stern, looking at Big Spencer looming over Caribou Lake when I thought I saw something dark skim over the water, following us at a distance. Darker shadows were catching up to us. I shook my head, not believing my own eyes, but when I looked again, Ki'kwa'jenu's black wings had disappeared. I so wished he would leave me alone.

After a while, Tommy Bridge joined me. It was nice to have someone closer to my age to talk with.

"What brought you here?" I asked. Tommy raised his head and looked at me.

"My brother and I don't have much of a future in Canning Town," he said.

"What's Canning Town?" I asked.

"One of the poorer parts of the city," he replied.

"You don't have family there?" I wondered.

"None who want to help us," Tommy sighed, looking down at his shoes.

"Aren't you kind of young to be a woods worker?" I asked him.

"Maybe," he said, "but we were hired to work in the kitchen. It was the only hjob open when we signed up. They needed two of us," and he waved his arm to mean the immigrants on board. "They seemed glad to have a pair who knew each other."

Father had fixed the searchlight and was back at the helm. Tommy and I were on the left side of the bow with Uncle Amos on the right. It was getting harder and harder to see in the fading light.

It was getting so cold. I was glad I wore my warmest, long coat. I would be shivering even more if I hadn't. I curled my fingers inside my mitts and wished I had brought a warm scarf.

The searchlight went out again. Father turned the helm over to someone I didn't know, someone who was nodding his head. I only heard the word, "experience." In a moment, Father was standing on the bow next to me, fussing with the search light at the center while an immigrant was at the helm. A loud *pop* made me turn my head to the stern and then an orange yellow ball of fire burst through the wheel house, incinerating the stranger at the helm, turning him into a pillar of orange flame and piercing screams. Shards of glass burst through the rear windows on either side of the wheel. Sharp splinters from the cabin followed right along, glass and pieces of wood impaling some of the immigrant woodsmen. A few pieces of jagged metal flew into the fuel barrels, shredding them first, and then those went up in yellow flames and black smoke. Everything seemed to happen at once.

"Abandon ship!" I could hear Uncle Amos yelling. "Into the water! NOW!" I could see some men jump from the side I was on, and I thought I could hear splashing on the other side.

Those quick to climb around the right side of the wheelhouse and had made it all the way to the bow escaped the exploding fuel drums. The *Tethys'* forward motion stopped short when the keel hit the edge of the submerged channel, catapulting men off the bow into the water, just short of the dry bank. But those who were caught in the confusion on the overcrowded cargo deck weren't so fortunate.

One rolling barrel of kerosene crashed top end first into three men, killing two instantly as it exploded and sending the third into the lake. Those on the other side of her rear deck had hit the water as the last barrels blew. There were screams of agony from the boat, from the water, and pleas for help on the shore. Two badly burned men were trying to hang on to some old, bleached out cedar roots, made smooth as glass by the erosion of wind, spray and dust, too slippery to hold on to with ice chilled hands that were getting more numb by the second.

Father grabbed me just as the side fuel tank exploded in an orange ball of flame, but when the *Tethys'* bow hit the submerged bank and stopped short, we both tumbled overboard. Although I had fallen through the ice two winters before and knew how cold the water could be, I was still shocked by the icy chill.

I sunk like a rock, my heavy winter cloak pulling me to the bottom. I felt the soft mud under me. On top of me was part of a new cast iron stove top that I had helped carry on board. I started to see stars, but none I recognized. My head felt like it was going to burst. Back lit by the fire above, Ki'kwa'jenu's black wings were coming at me, sharp claws pulling at my arms.

In the near darkness six feet down, I could make out a man with a white beard, wearing a gold crown, a green scale covered body and a fish's tail chasing away the wings. Father's strong arms pushed the broken stove top off me, and he got me to the surface. He grabbed me, put his arm under my chin from behind me, then he swam me to shore. I was coming around a little then, the stars in my head mostly gone. The wings, too.

After Father dragged me to shore, I saw flames coming out the cabin windows and the bow hatch. Flames licked at what was left of the green canvass canopy. Her stern was slipping under water, her bow probably stuck on the mud bank of the channel, coming to rest only a few feet from shore. Billows of thick, black smoke were everywhere. The choice for some, I later learned, was burn or drown. Very few of the men could swim.

"Help me," I heard someone shout, thrashing about, trying to stay afloat. Then I heard gurgling, coughing, and other voices in languages I didn't understand. Father was yelling to them. Some voices went quiet, then only the sound of the burning *Tethys* remained.

We were able to climb over a tangle of dri-ki, the tangled mess of bleached stumps and tree trunks left behind after the lake level rose with the new dam. We sat beside an old pine stump that the ice had pushed over on its side, its snarled, bleached roots snaking up to the cold sky as if they grew in the air. A few others climbed toward us.

"Swim over here, you'll be safe with us!" Father screamed, grabbing long, thin pieces of driftwood and throwing them at the struggling swimmers like life rings. "Grab on to it now!" he commanded, picking up another piece of wood to throw to one more man. "Kick your feet!" he yelled.

Several had already crawled up onto the shore with us. Uncle Amos and Louis were with them. I could barely make out a few more on the other side of the boat, only her bow out of water, flames licking the darkness. It became very quiet. The stillness made the hair on my neck rise, you know, the feeling you get when things are really, really bad. My pant legs had started to freeze stiff, and I couldn't easily move.

I was still a little groggy after Father pulled me to the surface. After I found a level log to rest on, I looked up next to me at an old pine tree with a dead top, apparently hit by lightning. There, on one of the branches, sat Ki'kwa'jenu, coal-red eyes drilling into me. He seemed to be smiling. I jumped up, shouting at the black beast.

"Get away, you don't belong here," I said. "Go away, go!" I looked around for something to throw at it, grabbed a smaller piece of wood and flung it at Ki'kwa'jenu.

"Charlie, what's wrong?" I heard Father ask, looking toward the pine. "There's nothing there, Charlie, it's okay. Just the cold playing games with your mind." The last thing I remember before I blacked out is being under a pair of black wings, grasped in sharp talons, disappearing into the Katahdin Range. When I came to, I was sitting up beside Uncle Amos trying to get warm.

"Let's get some kindling," Father said. "Amos, can you help? We'll put the fire right here." Someone had a jackknife and whittled away some shavings. Others broke up some dri-ki sticks. Only a few were able to help. The rest were too stunned from the explosion and the icy feel of their wet clothing to do much of anything except sit and shiver.

"How are we going to light the fire?" one of the survivors said. "No one has dry matches now."

"I have some," Uncle Amos said, pulling a dry box of matches from under his hat. He scraped some lichen from a nearby stump and placed it on the shavings along with a few pinecones. In a few minutes, we had a good fire going, the sweet smell of cedar surrounding us.

"Come over here, get warm," Father shouted down the shore to the others, some sitting on stumps like safe little islands. They would die there from exposure soon if they didn't find their way to our little fire.

"Amos, see if you and Louis can help some of them over here. Their legs must be numb from the cold by now." Several had already crawled closer to the fire, some having to get wet all over again as they lowered themselves off the stumps here and there where they had been sitting. Slowly, they waded over to us. I couldn't imagine getting back into that freezing water and getting soaked all over again, but if they didn't leave the stumps, they'd all freeze and soon. I counted seventeen again, just to be sure. Many had wounds from the exploding glass and wooden wheel house.

"We need more wood!" shouted Father. "Bring what you can over here."

"Can't we walk the shore to those lights?" asked one of the workers. From his question, I could tell he knew nothing about what the lakeshore was like. A tangled mess of stumps and logs made it necessary to climb over something every foot or two. And there were several inlets to cross, too. We'd have to get soaking wet again, more than once. We'd freeze to death if we tried. Ki'kwa'jenu was waiting to carry us away one by one.

"We're better off staying by the fire. This is our rescue signal, so stay close," Father said.

"Do you think they saw the flames from the Depot?" Louis asked Uncle Amos in a low voice. Father was fiddling with the fire, getting it bigger, getting it hotter I hoped.

"Hard sayin', not knowin', but I hope to Christ somone did," Uncle Amos answered.

"There's only one man at the Depot," we heard a voice say in the background. It was the camp clerk who had come back with us from a Bangor trip with Uncle Amos.

The clerk moved closer to the fire. "There aren't any canoes there either, and he's all alone," the clerk said. "If he saw us, he'll call over to the Village for help. God, it's cold," he said, shivering as he came closer to the fire. I could hear his teeth chattering. "I hope he saw us; I pray that he did, and that the phone works!"

"I was bringing in a new Bull Cook, but I don't see him here," he said.

"This is all of us," Uncle Amos said, his wet clothes steaming from the heat. The clerk looked away.

"How many?" Father asked Uncle Amos.

"How many what?" Uncle Amos replied. Father's jaw was clenched, veins bulging at his temples.

"How many missing?" Father must have sensed that not all would be accounted for. How could there be many survivors after that explosion? How could there be any?

I started to count the men. "There are seventeen of us here," I offered between chattering teeth. He just shook his head, the anger passing. I don't think I've ever seen him look so angry and defeated as he did right then. There was no sign of the rest, not a body, not a floating hat, nothing but an oily sheen on the water and a burning boat.

"That would mean fifteen or sixteen missing," Father was shivering from the wet and the cold. He didn't seem to be sure.

Those who escaped the explosion and fire were going to die from the cold or their injuries. And soon. I already couldn't feel my feet, and my hands weren't far behind. It was too cold to shiver. The smell of wet wool was everywhere.

Father stopped staring at his shoes and motioned for Uncle Amos to come to the edge of the firelight so the others wouldn't hear.

"That wasn't just a fuel explosion," Father said.

"Doesn't seem so," Uncle Amos said in a low voice. "When we were at the Dam, getting something to eat, I thought I saw one of Fanny's men walking back from the dock with a leather satchel."

"Why the hell didn't you say something?"

"Because he disappeared so fast, I thought I was imagining it. There were a lot of people milling about, unloading and loading other boats." He paused, and then said, "So I went on board and didn't see anything unusual, even asked a few who were standing around, but no one else had seen him. Now I think differently."

"If that's so," Father said, "it's war with Fanny." Uncle Amos, Louis and I looked at each other. I worried about what could be ahead, and I was also worried about how much Louis was learning about the business. Was Father bringing him in? It almost looked like it.

"Let's not jump to conclusions here," Uncle Amos said.

"Well, who the heck else could it be?" Father was close to spitting mad, just a notch below full boil.

Uncle Amos thought a moment. "If I were a general fighting a strong enemy, I might want someone else to whittle him down first, and then move in for the kill myself."

"What do you mean?" Father wondered.

"Remember the Boston gang Mike talked about?" Uncle Amos asked.

"Yeah, he did mention them."

"Well, if Boston did this but could make us think that it was Fanny, we'd go after her, and then...."

"We'd be doing Boston a favor," Father finished. He thought a minute. "Let's wait a bit to let this sugar out. Besides, if we don't get picked up pretty soon, it won't matter anyway."

We waited for rescue, sunrise almost fifteen hours away this time of year. As we huddled around that fire like it was the source of life, snowflakes began drifting down around us.

Chapter 12

A mile farther into Cuxabexis Cove was the Depot, our destination. I could see it from our perch on the dri-ki, a weak light in the distance. It was only a mile away, but it might as well have been a hundred. The tangle of stumps and old trees littering the shore and the three or four streams to wade across made a walk impossible for nearly frozen men.

In the Depot's mess hall, the cookee had probably finished his dinner early, expecting our arrival with a boatload of hungry men. I imagined him around the warm stove, planning our dinner, and I wanted to be there so bad. There had to be plenty of beans from the days before. He would be busy whipping up some biscuits, brewing some coffee, getting hot water ready for tea and seeing that the table had utensils, cups and stacks of plates. I'd give anything to be in that camp at this very moment. It would be safe, warm and peaceful.

....

The cooks were up at 3 A.M. brewing coffee, frying up bacon or ham and warming up the beans. They'd make donuts and loaves of bread. They'd fry up onions with potatoes. They would set out piles of tin plates and gray enameled cups beside the camp "silverware." More than once, I enjoyed a breakfast at one of those camps. I could use something warm inside me right now.

The cookee was about to drop his tin plate into the steel sink when he looked out the tiny window. A second earlier, the noise of the explosion had caught his attention. Now, bright orange and yellow flames were shooting above the tree line, backlighting the fir and spruce tops, and reflecting off the water. From where he watched, the fire seemed a mile away in the thoroughfare. As he reached for the hand crank Western Electric wall phone, he wondered if anyone had been hurt.

He cranked three long rings for the West Branch Boom House, four miles away, trying several times before getting through.

It was five p.m. and it was getting dark. Seventeen men had been trying to get warm around a dri-ki fire on the shore of freezing Moose Pond Stream for at least the last hour in lightly falling snow.

Chapter 13

"West Branch Boom House," Al Currier answered finally. Al was in charge of the Company's Spruce Wood Division, and he often stayed in the Boom House, the Company's headquarters at the first bend of the river just above the Village.

"This is Boras," Cookee said. "Caleb King's boat is on fire in the Thoroughfare. I'm alone at the camp, and don't even have a canoe to go help them," he explained.

"Put the hurricane lantern with the red lens on the dock," Al told him. "Then heat up some water for tea and make plenty of coffee. I'll get someone over there right off," and he hung up.

Al called his boatman a mile away in the village. This was the same phone line that Louis had just finished repairing. I wondered about Louis' being on the boat with us. It had always seemed somehow strange to me that the man who just fixed the phones was saved by them.

"Village Depot," Fred answered.

"Fred, Boras just called. Caleb's boat is on fire in the Thoroughfare," Al said.

"In back of Gero?" Fred asked.

"He said it was in the Thoroughfare, so I assume so. Can you gather up some warm blankets and get over there quick, see what you can do?"

"I'll leave right now," he told Al, hanging up the phone and pulling on his coat, his wool hat and some gloves. The snowshoes he had been working on would have to wait. Fred hadn't seen it as cold this season, and things were beginning to ice up. He was going to pull out the *Twilight* and settle her on her supporting cradle the next day, hiring

Caleb's ox team to drag her to high ground for the winter, but that might have to wait. He hoped there would be a few more days before the entire lake froze. Fred grabbed a pile of blankets from the bunk room and hurried down the path to the dock, thinking if he had followed his plans to retire last year, he wouldn't be taking his boat out on a lake that was starting to freeze over at the end of November.

After loading the blankets, he started up the four-cylinder, four-cycle Lathrop. At thirty-five feet, the *Twilight* had a full wooden canopy, much like the *Tethys*. Its motor developed over 90 horsepower at 1,500 RPM. With nearly 600 cubic inch displacement, there was plenty of power even with the heaviest of loads. Fred always took good care of his things, and this boat was no exception. He could depend on it.

With the boat loaded, Fred pointed the bow to south Gero. He was by himself, needing all the room he had for survivors. He knew a change in the weather was on the way as clouds had been dropping lower and turning slate grey all that afternoon. A few snowflakes hung in the air.

"They'll be frozen solid by the time I get there," he worried aloud, and gave the Lathrop more gas.

It was now past dark, and the thin skim of ice was slowly spreading over the calm surface between the Village Cove and the Gero Island Depot. Fred decided to cut the corner at the south end of Gero just a little closer to Gull Island, avoiding the longer trip down the spine of ledges that spread several miles south from nearby Gull. Fred knew the lake well. He kept careful watch for signs of Table Rock, just one hazard that was close to his route between Gero and Gull Islands. By the time he got to Gull, it had stopped spitting snow. He could see the glow of a small fire on the shore. This was the right place.

Fred turned on the spotlight just in case there were some pulp logs and deadheads in his path. He continued turning the corner, watchful for outcrops, and then saw the remains of the *Tethys* against the driftwood, her bow still burning, smoke and flames still on the water from the spilled kerosene, a multi-colored sheen reflecting from the spotlight.

Caleb was often overloaded with immigrant laborers recruited by the Company. As he got closer, Fred could see a small group on shore waving at him. Where were the others? He throttled down after a plaid shirt and red suspenders floated by. He had the answer to his question.

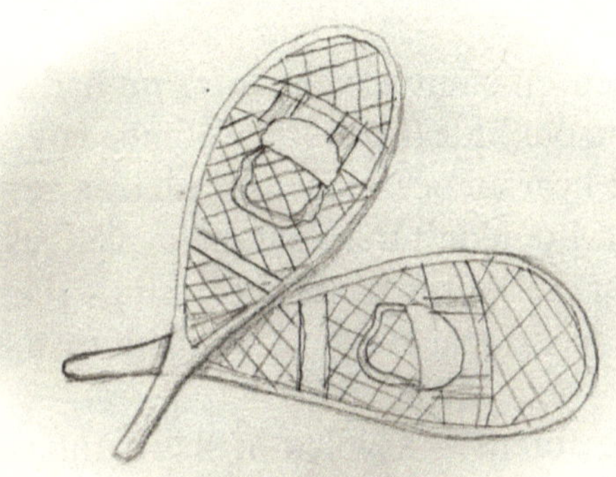

Chapter 14

"Can we get closer to the fire?" I asked Father who was staring at his shoes again. Tommy Bridge was huddled beside me. He was only two years older, and he was crying.

"Come over here, boys," Uncle Amos asked us. My pants had started to steam a little, and the feeling was coming back to my legs, but I was still shivering.

"Can you feel your legs?" Father wondered. "If you can't, you could burn yourself if you get too close," he warned.

"Has anyone seen my brother, William?" Tommy had been calling out William's name into the darkness for a while now. There had been no answer.

Men huddled in pairs, making it difficult to get much closer to the fire anyway. I thought it was strange that it was fire that put us here, but fire that kept us alive. I tossed that idea around for some time while we waited and waited for help we didn't really know would arrive in time. The smell of the burning *Tethys* was at times overcome by the smell of wet wool.

Hypothermia can set in when the air and water temperatures combine to less than 100 degrees. The water was close to 45. The air was less than 32. A few snow flakes didn't make it better. At least there was no wind to chill us even more.

Shivering is the body's attempt to stay warm, like an automatic form of exercise. When shivering doesn't help, the body goes into survival mode. Blood from the arms and legs flow back to the core to keep the brain, heart and other organs warm enough to function. If someone who fell through the ice was able to crawl out, they were often found naked, feeling very warm and removing their clothing just before the heart stopped.

Those who had been perched on stumps close to shore had to brave wading through the icy water to our little fire. As they climbed over the slippery, wet tree roots, I could hear an occasional splash as a few immigrants slid back into the water. I couldn't translate the expletives, but it wasn't hard to figure out that the words weren't blessings. The only other sounds came from an occasional *pop* and *bang* from the *Tethys*, her bow still smoking.

"When will someone come for us?" a voice in the darkness asked.

Uncle Amos looked in that direction, and said for all to hear, "I'm sure the fire has been seen." We hoped it had been seen, but we had no way of knowing when a boat would come. Some of the men didn't look so good.

"But what if it hasn't been seen? What then?" another voice asked.

"There's always boat traffic here," Uncle Amos lied. "It won't be long," he assured them. I knew he was lying to them to keep up their spirits. Our boat was the only one that came this way, maybe once a day, and it was burning right in front of us.

One man who had helped me load cargo at the Dam was stretched out beside the fire, groaning in pain. This guy was a good worker, never hesitating to heft a keg or offer me a hand with something heavy. He was a whistler. I had never heard the tunes he whistled before, but it was obvious he was a happy guy. Now he was laid out on the shore of a freezing lake in the snow, soaking wet with a big gash across one arm. One of the men was wrapping a kerchief around it to stem the bleeding. "He's stopped breathing!" I heard one of them shout. "Do something!" Uncle Amos stumbled over and placed his ear on the immigrant's chest, checking for breath. The chest was not moving. One of the immigrant wood-cutters had just died.

"He's gone," Uncle Amos said. Can't hear a heartbeat, and he's not breathing." No one spoke. Danger was everywhere in the woods here. A tree falling wrong, a log jamming you against a rock on the river drive, falling through the ice, or in our case, sitting on a log beside the lake soaking wet while it was snowing. The back of my coat had frozen stiff, but the front was steaming in front of the fire. The scene began to fade again, black wings dancing in the shadows. Ki'kwa'jenu was coming back, and I imagined he was coming for me. I almost passed out.

"Hey, I see a light moving toward us!" someone shouted. We looked up. A white search light got larger and brighter. It was the *Twilight*. I would have cheered if I wasn't so darn cold.

Chapter 15

We had been on shore for an hour when we saw the lights of the *Twilight*. Those who still had the energy began to shout.

"Over here!" several shouted together, waving their arms.

"Watch out for that deadhead!" another cried out.

"Thank God someone came to help," came from the back side of the fire pit.

Fred steered for the fire we had made, knowing he was at risk from the water hazards that blended into the dark. Throttling back, he passed the bow of the *Tethys*, the first five feet of her jutting out of the water, burning a little, smoking a lot.

Steering the *Twilight* to the side of the slippery, steep clay bank where we were perched, he cut the motor to an idle and drifted between two huge pine stumps, her side toward shore. I could hear scraping of submerged roots along her hull as she got closer, but she kept floating to us.

"Let's get all of you on board!" Fred shouted to us. "The camp's waiting for you with hot coffee."

Fred slid out a plank, placing it between his boat and the dri-ki. We came on board. Fred helped each one step over the gunwale on to a little riser, handing a wool blanket to every other survivor for the last mile's ride to the Depot at Cuxabexis. The men did not object to huddling under the same blanket. Father and Uncle Amos had to carry one with a makeshift stretcher, a blanket wrapped around two poles they found in the dri-ki on shore.

The whistler's body was the last brought on board. Fred carefully covered him with a canvas tarp.

When everyone was settled, Fred backed the *Twilight* away from the muddy bank, and steered towards the faint light at the Depot.

Cookee met Fred's boat at the Depot's dock. Boras grabbed the stern line thrown to him, quickly wrapping it twice around the dock's cleat, stopping the boat's forward motion immediately, bringing the *Twilight* against the bumpers. A second rope from the bow was thrown next, and Cookee scrambled thirty feet more to secure that one around the last cleat to pull in the bow so the passengers could climb off.

We began our shivering walk up the boardwalk toward the camp, a lantern on a post showing us the path. Cookie led us, and Fred followed the last one up.

"I haven't been this cold since those five winters in Siberia," I heard one say.

"Yah, but we were dry there," his friend replied. We walked into a toasty warm bunkhouse. Dry clothes from the Company's storehouse were soon brought out. Wet ones went on makeshift lines hung about.

When we were dry, we went into the dining area and sat at a long plank table where there was hot soup, warm beans, and hot coffee and tea. There was some conversation between the men, but I couldn't understand it until one of them began to translate for Father. As the captain of the disastrous journey, they seemed to hope he had some answers. He didn't. Cookee directed the men to help themselves, and then he attended to those who needed injuries looked at. There were cuts from flying parts of the *Tethys*. The burns were the worst. Some were still coughing from the smoke. Sheets were torn up for bandages. Uncle Amos made some wooden splints for a few broken limbs, and I helped with each one.

"Here, cradle your arm like this," I told my first patient, a burly guy who didn't understand English. Uncle Amos was sewing up a guy's forehead, leaving me by myself for splinting duty. For now, I tried to overlook Tommy's sobs I heard from the corner of the camp. I had to concentrate on splinting. The first aid class we had in school was a good one. Where we live, we had to take care of ourselves. Doctors could take a day or more to get here, depending on the weather and the time of year.

The next thing I knew, Father was on the phone to the hotel.

"We're okay," I heard him tell Mother. "Charlie's not hurt," he said. "He's warming up." Then he lowered his voice, but I could still hear him say, "I think we lost seventeen men."

"We'll come back tonight with Fred," he told her and hung up. Fred was next on the phone, telling Al about our trip to the Depot. When he finished with his report, he walked by the stove where Tommy was trying to get warm.

"My brother is still out there. Won't you please go look for him?" Tommy cried to Fred. Tommy was barely able to get the words out between his sobs.

"We will soon, young fella," Fred assured him.

Father looked at Tommy who had tears rolling down his cheeks and put his hand on his shoulder. "Fred will look for him on his way back after he takes us home. When he finds your brother, he'll take him back to the Village. I'll have him call us when he gets there. You should come back with us." That seemed to calm Tommy a little, and he nodded to Father's invitation.

Father decided that along with himself, Uncle Amos, Louis, Tommy and I would return to the hotel with Fred that night, along with a few injured men who could travel. It was decided the remaining survivors would be better off where they were, not having to brave an icy cold trip back to the hotel. It would be a couple of days before a doctor could get here if the lake hadn't frozen up and if one could be persuaded to make the trip.

As he approached the Thoroughfare where the *Tethys* rested, Fred throttled down in case he needed to avoid something floating. There was no sound coming from shore or from the islands of stumps nearby. We called out several times, sweeping the search light over the channel. Tommy called for his missing brother until he was hoarse, more distraught with each unanswered scream of his brother's name. Hearing and seeing nothing, we motored on.

Finding the Village in the dark wasn't a problem. Kerosene lights in the houses crowded around the cove's breakwater made it easier to see the town dock the closer we came. Fred tied up in the Village cove. In case a strong wind came up in the night, the *Twilight* would remain safely in the lee that stretched from Graveyard Point at the north end to the little point that ended the Village cove at the south.

Mother met us at the dock. She gave me the biggest, warmest hug ever, her hands grasping the blanket I had over my shoulders.

"I was so worried about you," she told me. "Are you alright?"

"I can't get warm enough." I couldn't seem to pull the blanket any tighter around me. "The lake is pretty cold. It started to snow." I told her how Uncle Amos was able to start a fire.

She turned to Father. "What happened, Caleb?" She asked.

"There was an explosion in the engine room," he said. "I think the engine backfired and set something off. It's just luck that any of us survived."

Father didn't tell her what he really thought caused the explosion. He was feeling powerless against an unknown and mostly unseen enemy. Father was uncomfortable not being in control.

Mother just looked at him. She sensed there was more to the story but didn't press for details. She turned away from Father. "There's hot cocoa and some soup on the stove," she said and pulled me closer with her arm around my shoulders as we walked up to the hotel. I was never so glad to be home as I was that night.

Chapter 16

After Fred got home that night, he rang Al. "I brought back seventeen survivors," he told him.

"How many are missing?" Al asked. Fred could hear the hesitation in his voice.

"Caleb thinks there are sixteen missing," he reported. Then he added, "but he's not really sure, could be seventeen."

"Round up six men and three canoes," Al instructed. "Get at least sixteen blankets and bring them all over to the wreck at first light. And make a signal flag for each canoe," he said.

"Blankets? The rest of them are dead, and what's a signal flag?" Fred asked.

"You'll need blankets to cover the bodies in the boat, and blankets will make moving them about much easier. The flag is just a white cloth on a stick," came the reply. "When the grapple snags a body, one of the men in the canoe will wave the flag. The recovery canoes won't be able to get the bodies inside them, too tippy. Once you see the flag, you'll motor over to pull the catch into the *Twilight*. Got it?"

Al had some experience with retrieval of more than one water logged body at a time. Once, he directed the search for four men who had gone under a log jam that had hauled unexpectedly. When those logs started moving, they also began to roll. They rolled right over the crew who tried to set them free. Their bodies showed up a mile down river at the foot of the rapids.

"Don't forget to bring along plenty of hot coffee and some lunch. You could be busy until dark. Ask Amos to make some grapples. It'd be quicker than doing it here."

"Amos was on the boat with them," Fred offered. "He just went inside to warm up."

"Well, since he's probably not up to it, we'll use the blacksmith up here and walk the gear down to you at day break." Al hung up.

It would be light enough at 7 to make the trip safely, and if any wind were going to rise, it would be after the *Twilight* had safely rounded the end of Gero. Fred planned to string the canoes nose to tail for the trip over and back.

We hung our wet clothes on the line in the back hall. Our boots went beside the cook stove. Father was shoving another piece of maple into the Atlantic Bull Dog stove in the parlor, and I was sitting in the kitchen, a blanket still around my shoulders and a cup of cocoa steaming between my hands when the phone rang. I answered. It was Fred calling for Father.

"Hey, Charlie," he said, "You feeling any better? How's Tommy?"

"I'm warming up," I told him. "Tommy had something to eat, then Mother took him upstairs to settle him in. He's pretty upset."

"Put your Dad on, will you?" he asked. I could hear breathing on the line and other noises that weren't coming from Fred's place. We had one big party line here. When the phone rang in one camp, it rang on every phone. Everyone was listening in. Mother told me that the phone had been ringing all evening, and not always for the hotel. The village grapevine was working overtime. For most folks who lived a quiet life in a place where nothing much ever happens, what was heard over the wire this night must have been spellbinding.

"Doin' okay?" I heard Fred ask. The phone was right beside the kitchen table where I was sitting.

"Somewhat, but I don't think I'm going to sleep much tonight," Father said. "Are you going back over to search tomorrow morning?" Father asked. Just then, Al knocked on the kitchen door and let himself in. He had walked down from the West Branch camp.

"Just as soon as it gets light enough to see," Fred told him. "Want to come with us?" I heard him ask Father.

"Someone needs to stay here with the men you picked up. Not sure what will become of the survivors. Wouldn't blame them a bit if they wanted out of here. Half of them can't even speak English," Father remarked. "I need to talk with the Company first thing in the morning. If he's up to it, I'd like to send Charlie with you."

"That's fine, Caleb. I'll keep an eye on him. Sometimes I think

I'm getting too old to be doing this, so it'll be good to have a strong back on board."

While Father finished his conversation with Fred, Mother was talking with Al. She had quite a scowl on her face. Just a few hours earlier, I had almost died. Father could have been killed if he had been at the wheel instead of the immigrant he drafted for the job. She didn't seem to like the idea of my going back to help with the search even though she knew that Fred would look out for me. I know she worried about Father. She shuffled back to the pantry for more coffee and sugar. Father, putting the phone back in the cradle, turned to Al and asked, "Are you going back with Fred tomorrow?"

"I need to talk with the Company and probably the sheriff, if he ever shows up. No, I won't be going. What about you?"

"I need to be here to check on the men. Some will want to go home, I suspect." Father looked at me, then to Mother, then to Al. "I'm really sorry this happened, Al. A hot coal from a pipe or a lit match must have set things off."

Father avoided mentioning the leaky gas line which would have made his lack of maintenance part of the cause. And he certainly couldn't mention the possibility that there was a bomb on board.

"Let's talk about this later on. As far as I know, it was an accident, wasn't it?" Why would he ask Father that? I wondered for a long time, and then decided that Al knew we had been running 'shine. He might have expected some trouble, but probably not this. I don't think Father did either, even though he had been warned. The puzzling thing was we hadn't done anything differently than what we had agreed to.

"Of course, it was an accident," Father said a bit too defensively. "There were a lot of lit pipes and cigarettes going. That's probably what caused it."

"Where's Amos?" Al wondered.

"Probably in his room in back of the store," Father said. Uncle Amos kept an eye on the store and had a little room in the back, but he took his meals with us.

"I've got a job for him tonight. I can't find the blacksmith at our depot up river, think he's on a toot or something with a bottle of that new Tanglefoot everyone's been drinking," Al explained. "Get some rest, Charlie," he said to me as he headed out the door to find Uncle Amos. I wondered how much Al really did know about our business.

In spite of his ordeal, Uncle Amos was up most of the night making four grapples, a tri-hook about a foot tall with the three hooks curving up eight inches and evenly spaced. There would be one for each canoe and one for the *Twilight*. The fourth was a spare. They looked like triple-hook fishing lures without the barbs. Uncle Amos forged a ring at the top of the grapple. After the iron cooled down, he added twenty-five feet of Manila hemp, the same rope adjusting tension on the wooden framed cross cut saws used for cutting spruce and fir. These were set aside for the morning's trip.

Mother insisted I go to bed early, but I tossed all night. I was up by 4 A.M. hearing Father fussing with the coffee pot at the kitchen sink and raking coals in the wood stoves. I came down stairs. Mother wasn't up yet. Neither was Tommy.

"Charlie, do you want to go with them?" Father asked.

"I'd like to go," I said. "I'm feeling a lot better now," I told him, hoping he'd let me.

"Better get some food in you. Mother will be down soon, and I'll instruct her to pack some lunches and coffee for everyone." Father put the coffee pot on the wood stove, stoking the fire with more birch.

"I think there's one of your brother's long coats in the upstairs closet. Your boots should be dry by morning. See if Tommy wants to come with you. It might make him feel better to be giving a hand." Then he turned and walked out of the room. I didn't think that pulling his brother's ruined body into the *Twilight* would make him feel better. I know I wouldn't.

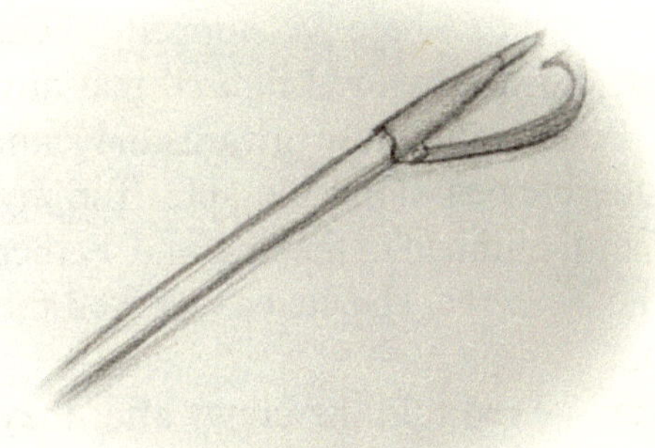

Chapter 17

By 7, it was light enough to start the recovery operation. Fred loaded the *Twilight*. The grapples, rope, flags and blankets were neatly placed in the tiny cabin below. Fred knew that the longer we looked at the gear, the harder it would be to do the job ahead of us, so he put a tarp over it. Six men were on board, and we left the cove in mirror calm water, towing a string of canoes, three paddles lashed inside each. Lunch had been loaded along with several thermoses of hot coffee.

Tommy came downstairs, wearing my brother's clothes. "Have you warmed up?" I asked.

"Much better," he said. "We wouldn't have lasted much longer when the rescue boat showed up."

"Good thing we had that fire," I offered. "I'm going back with Fred and some other men to see if we…" then I paused. I sensed I needed to be careful not to upset Tommy. I knew his brother had to be dead. I wasn't so sure he truly believed it. "…to see if there's anything we can find."

"I need to go," Tommy begged. "I need to find William. He must be nearly frozen solid by now."

"Let's find you some warm boots, a long coat, toque and mitts." We went upstairs to my brothers' rooms and found the warm clothes he needed. We never threw anything away, especially clothing. Mother thought that I might grow into the clothes they left behind and would never use again, so the pants, coats, work boots and shirts had stayed hanging in the closet ever since that telegram from the Adjutant General had arrived.

I knew that William Bridge would not be sitting on a cedar stump smiling and waving at us when we arrived. I wasn't so sure what

Tommy thought.

We reached the Thoroughfare by eight. The bow of the *Tethys* was just above the water and a little north of where we stopped. There was still a little smoke coming from the wreck. Fred figured that any current from the flooded-out Moose Pond would flow towards the Dam in a southerly direction. Bringing the canoes along the side, Tommy Bridge and his canoe partner, Sam Gero, climbed in the first one. Father told Fred to keep me with him on the *Twilight*. The canoes worked the Thoroughfare down the light current.

"Take these grapples and flags," Fred told the crews after they were settled in the canoes. One by one, they paddled over as Fred and I handed them the equipment they'd need for recovery.

"After you grab onto something, tie off the rope and raise the flag. I'll motor over and Charlie and I will do the lifting into the *Twilight*." It would be pretty hard to get a water-soaked corpse into a canoe without capsizing. Soon all the canoes were loaded up, and bowmen were casting for victims. I could see Sam steadying their canoe while Tommy threw the grapple.

Three white flags went up after a few casts. After we motored over to the first flag, we found it was Tommy who had snagged his brother's body. When we drifted close to their canoe, Fred and I took the rope, pulling the water-soaked corpse up beside the *Twilight*.

"Come on, Charlie, help me pull him out," Fred said. I'd never tried to pull a corpse into a boat before. I wondered if all bodies were just heavy or being wet made a difference. I could hear Tommy sobbing in the bow of his canoe.

"Be careful of him," he begged.

"We will, Tommy. We'll be really careful. Here, take this grapple," said Fred, "and look for more if you're up to it." Tommy had stopped sobbing, and with tears still on his cheeks on this cold November morning, he had accepted that William was no longer. I don't know if I could have done the same.

"I can do it," Tommy resolved, as much to himself as to us. He was pushing his grief to the back burner as I passed him the grapple. Tommy was keeping busy by pulling others out of the cold, impersonal waters of the lake.

"Bring me a blanket," asked Fred. I went into the cabin, brought out one of the dark green woolen camp blankets. I handed it to Fred.

He shook his head. "Unfold it beside him," Fred told me. I unfolded the blanket, and I placed it fully open beside the body.

"Now take William's feet while I take his shoulders and roll him over onto the blanket."

I was pretty sure that Tommy had seen only the uninjured side of his brother's head. I was glad I wasn't where Fred was. Half of William's face was gone. I could see his teeth where his cheek had been. Something whiteish grey showed above where his ear had been. He hadn't drowned; he was dead before he hit the water. His injuries came from the explosion. It was a good thing that Tommy decided to hang out with me and had moved towards the bow, or he would have died, too. Even though I had gutted plenty of deer, bear, pigs and sheep, I thought I was going to be sick at the sight of human brains.

We wrapped William up as neatly as we could and set him on the port side of the *Twilight*'s main deck. I helped Fred tie the blanket together in several places with some twine he brought along.

We were piling the bodies side by side until there was no more room to be respectful of the dead. We had to stack them on top of one another like the four-foot pulp wood they would never get to cut.

"Paddle over here!" shouted Fred to the crews, handing each boat a thermos of hot coffee and some biscuits as they floated beside the *Twilight*. "We have to go to the depot to unload, and then we'll be back in an hour." I could see Tommy shivering. His whole body was shaking.

"Tommy, you and Charlie come with us to help." Then, Fred turned to Tommy's stern man. "Sam, you come too. Tie the canoe on shore beside those cedar roots. I'll come pick you up." It was a tough call. Tommy was strong, willing, but he didn't realize he was getting too cold. He was shaking harder now, and he needed to warm up right away. Tommy stepped into the boat with his brother, both now wrapped tightly in warm wool blankets for different reasons. Later, when Tommy insisted on helping to carry his brother to the Depot storehouse for safekeeping, I was not surprised. Fred motored over to shore to get Sam. Then we delivered eight blanket-wrapped bodies to the storehouse just a mile away.

"Are you okay?" I asked Tommy. He stared at the remains of the *Tethys*, not responding to my question. I felt so bad for him. Leaving his family, traveling across The Pond, and fishing his brother's body from a strange lake in a foreign land, all within a month. I could tell he had had a rough life, that he knew things, had seen things that I couldn't imagine. Right then, I knew what I was going to ask my parents when we got home.

While we were making the delivery, the remaining crews hooked onto other victims, towed them to shallower water along the dri-ki, and tied them to islands of tree stumps to keep them from drifting away and sinking. It wasn't a cold job just because of the weather; it was a cold job because emotions had to be kept at bay.

By mid-afternoon, we recovered fifteen. According to the count that Father gave to Fred, we were missing one. There was no formal manifest, and there was no identification on half of them. Father wasn't sure how many immigrant laborers there were, and he relied on interviews with survivors to get a more accurate number.

"It's getting late," Fred said to me. It got dark by five this time of year, and we still had to get to the Depot and then travel all the way back home. "Come back over!" he yelled to the canoes. That afternoon, we had gathered up another seven victims. Some were so badly burned they didn't even look human anymore. I know; I saw each one of them as I helped Fred load them into the *Twilight*.

We tied up the canoes behind, nose to tail again. No one spoke on the ride back. There was no place to sit on the rear deck. Men stood, and a few were able to fit into the little cabin.

After we got back to the dock, I took Tommy to the kitchen to warm him up. Fred and the others walked to their warm camps. There was no warm camp for the seven in the boat and the eight at the Depot's barn. Some would remain forever unknown.

Fred left the bodies wrapped in blankets in the boat for the night. There was no point in moving those now, and they weren't going anywhere. No one stayed up to keep watch, but I imagine a few lamps burned in the camps along the cove where the bodies were rocked peacefully in the *Twilight* as babies were rocked in their mothers' arms throughout the Village.

It was a quiet meal that evening. Tommy didn't say much, and ate less.

"Tell us about your family in England," Mother asked.

"My parents are in the Whitechurch cemetery. We have an uncle who doesn't want us. William…." Tommy paused a moment. "William and I ran away to Liverpool, and we found a job on that steamer to Boston."

"There's no one back there who would look after you?" Father asked.

"No, no one." Tommy looked from him to Mother, then back to me.

"We were supposed to sail back on the steamer, part of the deal.

We would work both ways for a free passage on the next one."

"Why didn't you go back?" Father asked.

"We heard other boys had been cheated. They got all the way back, and then they were kicked off the boat with nothing, no pay, no ticket," he explained.

Father looked at Mother. Then they both looked at me. I wasn't going to have to ask that question; I knew what Father was going to say.

"Tommy, we've talked a little while you were resting. You're very strong, and not just muscle wise," Father said. "Mother, Charlie and I would like you to stay with us, live here, be part of our family…if you want."

"We've plenty of room," Mother said, "now that our two sons won't be coming home." She paused a moment, her eyes beginning to water. Sometimes grief is just there, just below the surface of everyday stuff. It doesn't take much to reveal it. "So, won't you be part of our family?"

Tommy's eyes brightened. "I'd like that," he said. "Thank you." He wiped a tear from his cheek.

"It's settled then," said Father. "We'll board you, look out for you, but you'll have chores to do, just like Charlie, understand?"

"Okay," he said, sounding like a response I would make to one of Father's instructions. *He's going to work out well*, I thought.

"Tommy, you know that William can stay here in our own little cemetery. We have some plots there, and we can let you have one for him if you want." Father could have a gentle and generous nature that was often buried under his stern exterior.

"I don't have any money," Tommy whispered.

"That's okay," Father assured him. "We can take care of everything, and you don't have to worry about it."

"We're going to turn in early," Mother said. "It's been a tough day for all of us. I'll make a nice breakfast for us tomorrow. It'll be waiting for you when you come downstairs, and then you and I should go through some clothes to see what will fit. There'll be plenty to choose from."

Tommy slept in the room next to mine, the one he had been in the night before. We went to bed, listening to the rising wind that was going to bring in a dusting of snow by morning.

As I fell asleep that night, I could feel something watching me. In my dreams I could see a pair of coal-red eyes on the barn roof. It looked like Ki'Kwa'Jenu was staying close. I didn't sleep well, dreaming of those black wings again, circling around the hotel, getting closer and closer. Once I dreamt that huge claws had grabbed Mother's calico apron from the clothesline, the apron strings streaming behind into a sky lighted by flames. When I woke up in a sweat, I could hear Tommy stirring next door. For the time being, I was relieved to know he was still there.

The next morning, Fred and Father went back to search some more. They found body sixteen after an hour's casting about with two grapples from the *Twilight*. Returning to the Depot, they collected the remaining blankets and took all the victims except Tommy's brother to Chesuncook Dam. The sheriff and four trucks were waiting for them when they arrived.

There was a conversation with Father, Fred and the sheriff. Nothing ever happened, no charges, no relatives demanding revenge. Sometimes I wondered why, after all the indignities already suffered by these nameless souls, such care was taken to lay them side by side, four to a truck, considering they had been stacked like pulp wood on the *Twilight* and in the Depot.

It was right after ice-out the next May when river drivers returned to Red Brook. On their way to the camp, a faded and torn red plaid shirt stood out against the bleached out, nearly white dri-ki on the shore. Evidence of burning told us that it was the last one, unknown, just like some of his fellow immigrant workers. That brought the total fatalities to seventeen, the same number of survivors. Most were buried in the Greenville cemetery in the Company's lot.

Chapter 18

Our new village cemetery still had empty plots. A few years before, when the Company built the largest private dam in the world at Ripogenus Rapids, Chesuncook Lake was raised another thirteen feet. The increased flowage did more than create most of the dri-ki clogging the shoreline. The Village had been told that the water level was expected to flood the graveyard on the point. A crew of strong village men moved the graves with shovels, picks, wagons and horses. It took them three weeks. I had just turned ten when the digging started. When the water finally reached its new level, the old cemetery was still two feet above it. Father later told me that the Company wanted that site for a summer driving camp. They knew all along where the water level would end up, but they wanted the Village to do all the work of moving the graves.

I asked Hiram about moving the bones as the lake came up to the edge of the old cemetery. He said it wasn't easy. Hi was the village grave digger and coffin maker. No one else wanted the job. It didn't seem to bother him, though, being around all that death. I was helping him dig the grave for Tommy's brother when I asked him about the move.

"The worst part was getting all of the pieces of pine coffin out of those graves. Bottoms fell out, sides caved in, and then there were the bones."

"Then what?" I asked him.

"Had to jump down in there and gather everything with a trowel, put them in a burlap sack, skulls, bones, metal belt buckles, coins that had been left on their eyes and toss them all in the wagon with what was left of the coffins. Had to keep track of who was who by placing the bag of bones on top of the headstone we had already loaded into the wagon. The hardest part was the children." I could see Hiram stuffing skulls and bones into the sacks and then throwing the burlap bags out of the sunken graves into the wagon. I hoped I wouldn't dream about it.

I threw more shovels full of dirt onto the growing mound above me.

"There were forty graves to be moved, including Antosha's stillborn twins.

"What happened?" I asked.

"Her husband had been cooking at a logging camp at Umbazookus when they were born, the coldest week of the winter. The poor things never drew a breath. There was only Blind Bill, their boarder, to help. He really could see just a little, but always wore dark glasses with shades on the sides. Antosha wrapped up the stillborn babies in an old shawl and kept them frozen in the wood shed until her husband returned the next month so he could see them. They never had other children."

I stopped shoveling for a moment and looked at him.

"This is hard country. Death is always beside you," Hiram told me, "hiding in your shadow where it can't be seen."

While we were digging, Hi told me the story of Kenu, the monster who would eat your bones to take any power you might have. It was not easy to escape Kenu, but sometimes he could be tricked.

"One day," Hiram said, "Kenu came across a woman making bread from acorn meal. 'You should give me some of that now,' Kenu told her. She knew who he was just from how he smelled and from seeing his bright yellow eyes. But she knew what to do to keep him from eating her. 'It will be ready soon,' she told him. 'While I finish, why don't you warm yourself by the fire?'"

"Kenu moved toward the fire, and while he had his back turned, the woman mixed a special powder she had kept just in case he came by. The powder had come from the roots of a plant that grew only on an island in the roughest rapid on the river."

"What was the plant?" I asked.

"The plant ate flies, and I remember that it looked like a pitcher, but I don't remember its name. She mixed some of the powder into the acorn flour, and then she baked the bread. 'Here,' she said to Kenu, 'Have this bread,' she told him."

"What happened?" I asked.

"The powder put Kenu into a deep sleep, giving the woman time to pack her basket and run to the next camp."

"But wouldn't Kenu follow her?" I asked.

"No. The powder made Kenu forget, and he moved on to someone else's shadow where he might not be seen until it was too late."

Kenu was always around. He was there for my Uncle Charlie when he was returning from checking his trap lines one March across the Caucmagomic hills. Father told me the weather had turned warmer than usual, and there had been some rain, raising the water and undercutting the ice over Caucmagomic Stream where his brother had to cross. He should have known, Father said, but Uncle Charlie tried crossing it anyway. He broke through the rotten ice half way across. Whether the current carried him under the ice sheet, or he just numbed up and sunk out of sight, I'll never know. But I do know how cold it must have felt. Father said they found him on the north end of Gero in May. Hiram is right; Death hides in your shadow.

The ground hadn't frozen much yet. Maybe the first inch or so, but that was easy enough to break through. While Hiram and I dug the grave, Tommy stayed in the hotel with Father and Mother. Father helped Tommy place his brother in the simple pine coffin Uncle Amos had made, saying a prayer or two with the local minister who arrived on horseback for the service.

"Why here, Hi?" I asked as we entered the new cemetery.

"Got a nice view, don't it?" We looked back down the hill where we could see over the church belfry with the wooden white cross on top. Gero Island was in the background, and Katahdin stood out directly to the east. To the south was the top of Big Spencer. The fields along the lake shore went back over a thousand feet from the water and stretched south for over two miles with few groups of trees. I could see the four farms on Gero, open fields and barns. The Company's Gero Depot was right across the lake. The *A.B. Smith* sidewheeler was at her dock, smoke stacks quiet, waiting to be pulled on to her winter cradle until next spring's drive. We were looking at a panorama of man's determination to cut down all the forests as fast as possible.

"Some wanted to have the cemetery at the other end of the Village. There's a nice sandy spot there, good drainage, but this is what the elders chose. Politics, I guess. When we dig a grave in May, soon as the frost's out of the ground, we have to put pine boughs in the bottom before the hearse rolls up the hill."

"Why?" I asked.

"Because the boughs cover up the water that seeps into the grave.

Folks planted here a few years ago must be pretty well drained down to the lake by now." Hiram looked at me and smiled. "Come on, let's get busy." I guess making light of death was his way of keeping it back in the shadows.

We dug forever it seemed, Hiram on one end, and me at the other. There was mostly clay, a few small rocks, but hard digging. We made a little ladder with fir logs, one shorter than the next, lined up side by side, straight up. The different heights were like steps. I had to step out so Hi could use the pick to break things up, then hop back down to help him shovel out what he had managed to claw out of that hard, orange clay. Getting in and out of the grave wasn't easy. It was nearly six feet deep by the time we had had enough. After Hiram climbed out, I handed him the logs. He extended his huge paw to pull me out. We placed pine boughs on the bottom. The water was already starting to pool. Hiram covered up the pile of dirt at the grave's foot with an old tarp.

"Why are we covering the dirt up?" I thought to myself. Apparently, I said it aloud as Hiram replied,

"All creatures are different about death of their own kind," he said. "People like things neat, clean. Not seein' is not knowin'. That's why the dirt's covered up." Hiram put his shovel down as we were ready to put the boughs in the bottom. Hi hopped back into the empty grave. I started handing him the pine boughs we had cut earlier.

"Take geese, for example. They pair up for their whole lives."

"Father and Uncle Amos shoot geese," I said. "They make a good meal."

"One day, I shot one," Hi said. "It was flying with about twenty others when it fell out of the sky to the shore." I remembered seeing geese in flocks of a hundred and more, lifting off Brandy Pond whenever we went fishing there in the fall. "Here, hand down those two." I passed him two more pine boughs, just wide enough to fit, leaving room for the coffin.

"The rest of the flock turned around and landed by the fallen goose," Hi continued. "They sniffed it all over, and then they all flew away. That was how they understood death. Maybe we should just sniff and, in our case, walk away."

I passed him the rest of the boughs, and then I gave him my hand as he climbed out. When I grabbed his hand, I noticed that both of us needed a little cleaning up, but it was too late for that.

Just as Hiram finished the story and crawled out of the grave,

Duke, the roan Father kept around in case the truck wouldn't run, or when it was too muddy in early spring, brought the hay wagon with the coffin into the cemetery. The minister, Uncle Amos, Mother and Tommy were walking behind.

The minister led the train. Tommy was behind him, head down. He had on some of my older brother's best clothes. I remember the vest he used to wear. You could see he had been crying. Mother walked beside him with her arm around his shoulder, holding him as close as she could while still being able to walk. Behind them was Uncle Amos, wool hat down to his ears, red suspenders showing around his open winter jacket.

A cold wind was building, and it looked like some weather soon. We needed to hurry so we wouldn't be outside if it started blowing hard. I helped Hiram, Uncle Amos and Father with the pine box, sliding it carefully off the wagon onto the ground. Using two ropes, two of us to a side, we lowered it down onto the pine boughs. I felt sad for Tommy; I knew how he felt. I was glad that we could do this for his only brother. Some words were said, Tommy cried a little, Mother comforted him, and after shoveling back the dirt, we all rode back to the hotel in the little wagon, Duke plodding along the way he always did. The gravestone would be ready in the spring. For now, a plain wooden cross marked William's grave.

We rode back to the barn on the wagon, Duke pulling carefully on the slippery hill. Uncle Amos and I had to get back to make more 'shine.

I would have a few more visits to the cemetery before the next summer ended.

Chapter 19

The next morning, as Father made a second pot of coffee, Uncle Amos knocked and walked in. I was sitting at the kitchen table, finishing my breakfast. Tommy had started his chores, cleaning out the sheep pen in the barn. Mother was somewhere, probably making beds.

"Have a cup?" Father asked. He put in the fresh cream, and filled the thick, heavy mug. Handing it to Uncle Amos, Father said,

"Thanks for the help yesterday with the coffin. You didn't have to."

"The reason a grave had to be dug starts with you and me. I helped because I feel somewhat responsible, I guess." I think I stopped breathing a moment.

"Amos, we're going to have this talk once, just this once. Got it?" Father's face showed that stern 'I really mean it or there'll be a big problem coming your way by my hand or belt' expression. His face was getting a little red, too.

"Charlie," Father looked at me. "You need to hear this, and I don't want your mouth open. Flies could get lost in there the way you look right at this moment." I closed my mouth and nodded my head.

"This family is providing for itself. There's a market, a demand, and good money, really good money." Father drank some of the coffee he poured for himself after handing the first cup to Uncle Amos. "What other people do is on them. Not us. We didn't make that boat explode! Damn government put us here in the first place with their stupid law." Prohibition never had been popular in the village.

I hoped Tommy was still out in the barn and that Father's rising voice hadn't caught his attention. Mother was two floors up making beds and cleaning rooms, so she wouldn't have heard.

"If we hadn't gotten into the business, those men would be alive right now," Uncle Amos said in a level voice. He would often be calm when Father was a little hot. Sometimes, I couldn't tell if he spoke in that relaxed manner of his just to make Father angrier or to calm him down.

"True, and if I hadn't used that boat, they'd be alive, too. But I did. We can't take it all back, Amos. That wagon has left the yard."

"No," he sighed, dropping his shoulders and his head a little. "You're right. We can't."

"Then there's a practical matter, I suppose you want nothing to do with?"

"What matter is that?" Uncle Amos asked. My eyes went from one to the other, not wanting to miss anything.

"Money." Father took out a small black notebook. Using his pencil, he checked off numbers as if to add them up again, his lips moving a little. "We have enough to buy a whole township and the potato farm. We've been making 'shine for nine months as of last week. That comes to $2,400 each week. Deduct $400 for our costs and payoffs to the law, that's $2,000 a week for 36 weeks. We have $72,000 stashed away. The Company paid for the transport, but they don't need to know that."

"I hope you're keeping the money in a safe place," Uncle Amos said.

"It's in a safe place, Amos. No one is going to find it."

"So, if something happens to you, what then?" he asked.

"I showed Grace where it is, just on the outside chance that something might happen to me."

When eggs cost twenty-five cents a dozen and gasoline eight cents a gallon, Father and Uncle Amos had saved a fortune. And a township? A family could do well enough just cutting the timber and planting potatoes in the fields after the stumps were pulled and the soil tilled and rocked.

"I've found a nice potato farm that might be for sale at seventy dollars an acre," Father reported.

"Including buildings, equipment and critters?" Uncle Amos asked.

"Just the buildings and land. Usually the equipment and animals are sold separately, and it might be best to start with a fresh herd we know the details about and new equipment we won't have to keep fixing all the time."

"How big is that farm?" Uncle Amos asked.

"Just over 500 acres. We'll have enough to cover the land, the buildings, new equipment and a fresh herd if we want. And there's a neighboring farm that may be for sale there soon."

"What if I want my share and not buy a farm?" Uncle Amos asked.

"Up to you. Half is yours, like we agreed. Want to take it with you now or leave it with me?" I remembered overhearing him talk about a strong box he kept hidden under the floor boards in their bedroom. I kept quiet, watching the exchange and accurately predicting the outcome. Father had known all along what his brother would say.

"Better keep it safe," Uncle Amos sighed. "We'll keep at it; like you said, it's good money." With that, the lives of seventeen immigrant laborers were tied in a neat bundle and tossed away, like a dirty shirt thrown into the wicker laundry basket in the darkest corner of the closet. Suddenly, I was not feeling well. It was simple greed that drove Father to rum running. And I think there was a good measure of thumbing his nose at the Feds at the same time.

There was a tension in my gut, the same anxiety when you see something coming right at you, but you can't avoid it.

That feeling in the pit of my stomach was also part fear. It reminded me of how I felt when Father and Uncle Amos were nearly killed the year before. They had been driving long logs together. It was the only winter work before moonshine. As I was watching them work, the pile they were working on started rolling into the river towards them while they were balancing on some others already floating along the shore. It's never a good idea to be running across giant pine logs, end to end, while they're moving in the currents, but that's what they had tried to do.

Even with wearing caulked boots, those tiny nails all over the sole for a better grip, each had slipped and disappeared into the cold water under the logs. I was pretty scared, and I shouted after them. There was nothing I could do, no rope to throw, no one around to help. For just a few seconds, there was just enough space created by the currents for each to crawl out of the river, climb on top of a log, and to continue running towards shore as the logs rolled into the whitewater, closing the space they had to climb out from. I was scared then; I didn't like how I felt now.

"There's one more matter." Father reached for the sugar bowl.

Uncle Amos raised his head, sighed and took a sip of coffee. "What's that?"

"About the explosion. We don't know for certain who was behind it," Father said.

"Why would Fanny want to put us down?" Father said as he looked hard at Uncle Amos. "We made good 'shine, sold to her for a good price, and we're a major supplier. It doesn't make sense."

"Maybe it was someone else who hired it out?" Uncle Amos asked.

"But who? Unless….." Father paused a moment. "Unless another outfit wanted to hurt her by removing us from the mix? You think that Boston gang could be responsible?"

"That's a possibility, isn't it? Remember how we talked about this when we were wet and freezing, praying for rescue that night?" Might be a good idea to keep an open mind, at least until we learn some more." Uncle Amos was one to be cautious. Father was apt to bull ahead because he thought he was firmly in control. He wasn't. Not always. And not now. "They could have hired Feather-Man. Maybe he was their spy."

"Maybe," Father agreed. "And I have a plan to find out for sure. Meanwhile, we'll run the still all winter, sled it all to the Dam by the middle of March, and ship in May when the roads have dried up." Father poured himself more coffee, offering some to Uncle Amos who shook his head. "By the way, I hope you agree to split the cost of the new boat."

"Cost? What boat?" Uncle Amos was puzzled. I was, too.

"The business cost me my boat. The business, by that I mean you and me, need to replace it." He put his coffee cup down a little harder than usual. I could tell he was getting irritated again.

"Got a boat in mind?" Uncle Amos asked.

"Fred's gettin' done. He sold me the *Twilight* for $500."

"Sounds good."

"Seems like a good deal to me, too. We'll pull her up into the barn for some hull work this winter, and I think we should check the prop, too. We should look over her winter cradle tomorrow in case it needs some work before we pull the boat out of the lake."

"Time for me to get to work." Uncle Amos got up, put on his coat and headed to the barn to light the still.

Raising his voice to his brother's back, Father said, "I'll send Charlie out as soon as we've finished our little chat." I looked down to my empty plate again, wishing I was shoveling manure with Tommy.

"Charlie," he said. I looked up at him. He didn't seem mad at me, so I straightened up just a little. "You want to be damned sure you never ever repeat what you just heard between me and Amos."

"I'll be sure," I said. He seemed satisfied. Better to be out in the open, I thought.

"Now go help your Uncle Amos with the still." I got my winter boots and coat on and headed to the back of the barn where I could see a little smoke drifting from the chimney from the southeasterly winds. It had snowed a little the night before, and it was about to again this morning.

Chapter 20

Winter had settled in and so had Tommy. Christmas was coming up, and it would be hard on both of us, having lost our brothers. I kept busy working the still with Uncle Amos several days a week. We were either bottling, cleaning or cooking each day I spent with him. I was learning how to make the different types as well as how to age it in oak barrels.

Tommy was working for the Company while he lived with us, learning how to drive the sprinkler, icing the roads. Late in December, he asked me to join him on his night ride. Tommy and I hadn't spent much time together lately, me working the still, him driving some supervisor around in a sleigh, then working the sprinkler most of the night. My long johns, heavy pants, wool sweater and winter boots went on pretty fast. My life had become too predictable, and I welcomed any change to the routine. When I grabbed my hat and gloves and started to the door, Mother called after me. There was no one within earshot.

"I'm concerned about Tommy. He's been so quiet. See if he has something on his mind and let me know?"

"Okay," I said. Mother must have been really worried. She had never asked me something like that before. I started out the door again.

"Charlie, wait. You forgot this," she said and handed me a lunchbox with some bread, cheese, an apple and a thermos of hot coffee and gave me another warm hug.

Tommy and I walked out to the sprinkler rig. Tonight, just me and Tommy would run it, fill it, and run it some more. The Belgians had to be hitched up to the sled. Bred as draft horses in Europe, these were a bit shorter and stockier than Clydesdales. We had the only pair in the

103

village. The Belgians had a kind and gentle disposition. Uncle Amos hadn't docked their tails, so we had to be extra careful not to get them tangled in the pulling harness. The special ice shoes on their feet gave them needed traction on the slick haul roads. Once we got them hitched up, we were off to get the first load of water.

The winter roads were solid ice with two grooves like wagon tracks for sled runners to track in. Teams of horses could haul heavy loads of pulp, one sleigh bed hooked behind another. Once a load of wood got going, it was hard to stop. Sometimes we worked as road monkeys, shoveling gravel on the steeper sections to slow the loads down, and sometimes we shoveled manure off the track to keep the haul roads as slick as possible.

The sprinkler was a huge tank on skids on the back of a low sled. I hated it the minute I saw it, and I kept hating it ever since. Cold, wet, frozen, and miserable are only a few of the words I could use to describe the experience. Then there were the new adjectives and nouns I'd been learning from Tommy. 'Bloody' seemed to be his favorite. There was a large hatch on the tank's top and some bracing above where a pulley and rope hung. Our first job was to fill the sprinkler tank.

We urged the horses to back the sled up to the edge of a pond. Then we chopped a hole in the ice a little larger than the tank. I scrambled to the top to open the hatch and secure it so it wouldn't close by accident. Resting on two long poles, the tank slid off the sled and into a hole in the ice we had just opened up with our axes and ice-saw. Using the same poles, we pushed the tank under water until it filled. Tommy unhitched the team from the cart, set the brake on the sled, and hooked the rope from the tank over the pulley to the front ring of the sprinkler. The Belgians then pulled on the rope. The sprinkler tank slid out of the pond, up the poles and onto the stationary sled. I put the rigging away while Tommy closed the hatch and hooked the team back to the cart. We were off to sprinkle water on the roads.

When we got to the starting point, I'd knock out the little cork plugs along the bottom of the tank in the back. These dangled on strings beside each small hole like icicles dripping from a roof's edge. The dribbling water would make a freshly iced road for the next day's haul, smooth and fast. By spring, there'd be a foot of solid ice on the haul roads and bare ground everywhere else. If the road monkeys shoveled too much sawdust to slow the sleds down on the hills or didn't pick up the manure, the ice surface would be insulated from the hot sun and wouldn't melt until the first of June.

We were swaying back and forth. The Belgians were straining on the harness. Tommy turned to me, and said,

"Sometimes I'm as cold doin' this as I was the night William died and wonder if I'll ever be warm again." I looked at him, not knowing what to say. "Did Caleb ever figure out what started that fire?" he asked. He called Father by his first name, just like Mother and Uncle Amos did. Even though he was kind of adopted, he wouldn't call him "Father."

Although I knew what probably triggered the explosion on the *Tethys*, I couldn't tell Tommy. I felt I should say something, or he'd keep asking, and maybe he'd bring it up to Father which wouldn't be good. I wondered why he was suddenly asking and hoped he hadn't made the connection between the moonshine and the explosion.

"I think it might have been a pipe or a smoke," I offered. "There were barrels of gasoline at the back and the fuel line was a little leaky. It's a good thing you weren't sitting in the stern with the others." I sensed that he was still grieving for his brother, and that's what Mother had picked up on before she asked me to see if anything was troubling him.

Tommy looked at me again. I could tell he wasn't satisfied with my suggestion. He had been keeping an eye on the team as we were heading down a slight grade and needed to keep them reined in.

"That doesn't make sense. The first explosion came from the engine room, not the back of the boat by the barrels."

"No one seems to like my theory. Uncle Amos did say it could have been a leaky fuel line in the engine room. Gasoline fumes were set off by one of those backfires we heard off and on coming up the lake. That old motor did like to fart a bit," and Tommy nodded his head. He seemed satisfied for now.

"That makes more sense. I've been thinking about it once in a while, but that night is pretty hard to revisit." We were turning a corner and had started climbing a little rise with a long straightaway before us. "How much 'shine do you think we're making?" Tommy helped out, but not every day, so he wouldn't know really. I wondered why he was asking.

"More than a few cases a week when the stills are running is what I figure." I knew that was half the production, but I didn't really want to talk about the business. "Uncle Amos is storing it in the big shed. Some is aging in oak barrels we made. Guess there'll be a couple of big deliveries in May when the roads firm up. Maybe you can come along when we do?" The brightness of the mid-winter full moon made the woods look like mid-day. We could see long, dark shadow lines of the trees, stumps, and boulders as we passed. It looked like someone had taken a thin brush and painted black lines all in one direction throughout the woods.

Just then, a cutter pulled by one horse appeared from around the corner barreling straight for us. There was nowhere for us to go. Tommy pulled in the reins, shouting for the Belgians to stop. We were heading up a small hill at a wider place in the trail at that moment, but our load was too heavy for us to get out of the way. The cutter jumped the tracks, skidded sideways on the ice road to the trees, coming inches beside us. I got a close look at the face of the driver. There was no recognition, no expression, as she looked straight ahead, a pretty face surrounded by red hair fluttering behind her like a flag in a hurricane.

"Hey, are you crazy?" Tommy shouted at the disappearing rig. It took a moment for me to stop trembling, longer for the Belgians to calm down. Tommy slapped them lightly with the reins and we were moving again.

"Seems she doesn't like the 'go-back' road," I managed to squeak out. The winter haul roads were one way. There was a different road for the empty trip back. It was slower, rougher, but traveling over it was safer with one-way haul traces.

"Know who that was?" I had no idea.

"Not sure. Might be the new school teacher. Hope she has more sense about teaching than driving the wrong way on the haul road." Tommy was talking to the team to calm them down.

When I looked back into the darkness, I thought I saw something black following behind, but whatever it was, it blended with the shadows. The moon had disappeared behind dark clouds. We plodded on. I'd find out who she was when we got back.

Chapter 21

The weather turned even colder in mid-February. Spit froze before it hit the ground. Father said that meant it was close to fifty below. The lake ice made loud booming noises from time to time as the lake ice contracted. The snow squeaked when walked on, like a wild animal in pain. There was a haze in the sky from the blowing snow that filtered out the warmest rays of the sun. The thermometer didn't work after minus thirty-five, and I could feel the cold penetrating my clothes. My cheeks would sting as soon as I stepped outside, and it wouldn't take long before numb fingers and toes became frozen. Howling winds from Canada would not let up. I couldn't see the barn from the kitchen window. Some folks strung a rope between the back of their house to the barn to guide them so they wouldn't wander out of sight and freeze to death, but we didn't have to. There was a long, connecting shed to walk through. We didn't do much on those super cold days unless it was to take care of the livestock in the barn. Pigs had to be fed, stalls mucked out, our two cows milked twice a day. On these very cold nights, Father would keep a small fire in the Atlantic Bull Dog stove in the barn to help out the critters a little.

We were working the still. Uncle Amos was fussing with a new corking machine he had made.

"No, put that over here," Uncle Amos said, directing Tommy's efforts to clear a little space so we could begin bottling.

"We nearly got run off the haul road," Tommy offered. I hadn't wanted to bring it up. If I showed any interest in that incident, it would mean that the pretty girl driving was my focus and I would be teased with no mercy. Tommy and Uncle Amos would see it instantly.

"What happened?"

"Night before last, Charlie and I were icing the haul road when this cutter came skidding around the corner right at us, full speed."

Uncle Amos tilted his head and furrowed his brow. "You know who it was?" he asked.

"I'd recognize the driver of that cutter anywhere, but I don't know her."

"She had long, red hair and freckles," I interrupted. Darn! I should have kept quiet but couldn't seem to help myself.

"Ah, then you met Jim Ross' daughter, Abby."

"She lives here?" I asked. I thought I knew everyone in the village.

"She does," Uncle Amos said. He was then silent. He was making me work for it!

"And where might that be?" I dared ask, knowing the more questions I asked, the more interest I was showing. That meant more teasing.

"They live beside the clerk's camp at the West Branch Boom House on the point, just up the river. Know it?" Of course, I knew it. It had started already. I was doomed.

Tommy just smiled at me and kept re-stacking cases of bottles. We worked without speaking until Mother opened the barn door with some warm muffins and hot coffee.

"Charlie has a sweetheart," I heard Tommy say.

"A sweetheart?" Mother asked.

"Seems he met her on the haul road while he and Tommy were working the sprinkler the other night. Damn near ran them off the road," Uncle Amos added.

"Charlie, I had no idea," Mother said. "You'll have to bring her by. I'd love to meet her.

"You already have," Uncle Amos said.

"Yeah, she's Jim Ross's daughter, Abby," Tommy added.

By now, my face was so red it looked like I was on fire. I kept up with the bottling machine work while this was going on, and tried to ignore their conversation. When I turned to look at her, I saw a kind smile on Mother's face as she left the barn.

....

Louis moved into the hotel with us. It was the end of February, and he had nearly exhausted his firewood supply at his camp. I hadn't seen much of him the past few months since he was running his trap lines. Now, instead of cooking for himself, he was doing well enough to have Mother do it for him.

Uncle Amos was the fur buyer in our village. There were lynx, martin, fox and beaver carefully tagged and piled in the storage room. He told me that he'd do very well when he took them to market in Bangor in the spring when the roads had dried out. One day Louis brought in a pile of bear hides to sell. I helped him carry them into the barn.

"Been workin' on this pile for a bit," Louis said. "These are all good hides, no moths, no rot, all scraped and salted well." Uncle Amos looked them over.

"What do you want for these, Louis?"

"I was expectin' $200," his voice rising a little as if he were asking a question. Uncle Amos looked over the hides again. I could see they were well scraped and salted.

"They're good size, Louis, except for one. I can give you one-eighty for the pile."

"They're worth two hundred," asserted Louis, trying to stand his ground.

"Maybe they are, but not here. I'll go one-ninety." Louis sighed and nodded, the bargaining done.

"Want store credit or the money?"

"I'll take the money. Goin' down river, need it there," Louis said.

"Right," acknowledged Uncle Amos. "You'll spend most of it on Fanny's girls at the Nighthawk and drink the rest. Better get a round trip ticket so you won't have to walk home." Louis raised his eyebrow, didn't say a word, put the cash in his pocket, turned and walked out the door.

I helped Tommy lug the hides into the barn's fur storage room specially made to hold hides. It was nearly airtight. It had a painted grey wooden floor, walls and ceiling with one lantern hanging at each side as you walked through the heavy door. There was a stout bar across the door with iron fittings and a heavy padlock. The pelts were like deposits in the local savings and loan, neatly piled and waiting for Uncle Amos to find a fur buyer for his cache.

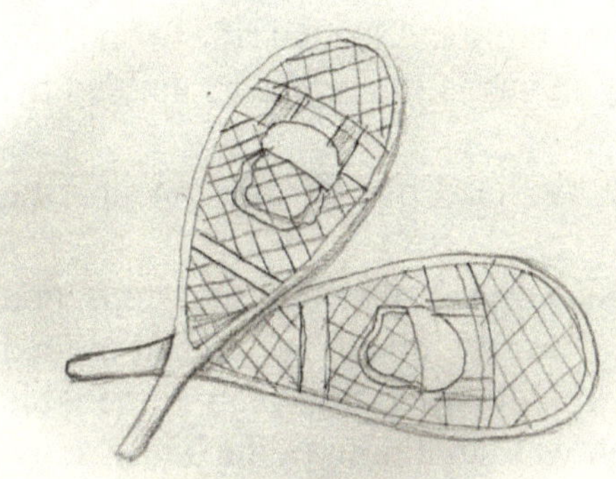

Chapter 22

We worked the rest of the coldest winter on record. Tommy ran the sprinkler, sometimes with my help. We both made more Tanglefoot. Uncle Amos found enough copper in the Village to make another still. We had three good ones to run at the same time with one always down for repair. And did we run them. I noticed when Tommy helped with the stills, there was something about his attitude that told me he didn't want to. I wondered if it seemed to him, as it did to Uncle Amos and me, that the family business was the reason for his brother's death.

When we had a little thaw in the middle of March, I took some time off after lunch and snowshoed down to see Hiram. There was something I had to ask, and only Hi would know the answer. I was using the bear paws we made just a few weeks ago. Steaming the split ash, bending them around the forms was the easy part. Lacing in the webbing was the hard part. The bear grease had soaked into the moose hide strips we used for the webbing, making the mesh somewhat waterproof. Otherwise, the webbing would saturate, soften and then sag, failing to give as much support on the snow.

When I got to the edge of the clearing, I headed towards his cabin tucked up against a tall stand of spruce trees. Hiram had dragged his home across the ice from one of the four farms on the island. I could see smoke drifting away from his fieldstone chimney and Hiram sitting at the table in front of the window beside the door.

"Hello the camp," I shouted. An odd expression, I have been told by flatlanders. In our world we address the camp, hoping someone is inside, not knowing exactly who might be there, and we do it from a little distance to give them a moment to respond, dress, load the shotgun or whatever they needed to ready themselves to receive a visitor properly. We don't do much visiting here beyond family. A loaded rifle or shotgun leaned against nearly every doorway in case foraging bears ambled by. Or other unwelcome visitors.

Opening the door, Hi stuck his head out. "Come on up," he invited. "Coffee's almost ready."

I kicked off the snowshoes at the bottom of the steps and stomped the snow off my mukluks. The strengthening sun had melted most of the snow and ice on the deck. Hi pointed to a chair at the table and poured each of us a cup. The sun was streaming in the big window beside the table. Strings of traps hung from the walls. Fishing rods were neatly hung from their tips on tiny nails. A canoe was suspended by ropes hanging from the rafters, just high enough to walk under without hitting your head. Inside a warm cabin was the best place to keep a canoe during the winter, out of the weather and handy for a quick repair or two. There was a collection of kerosene lights, suspended from an old wagon wheel that hung from the roof's peak by a rope. It was on a pulley and could be lowered to light the lanterns and raised to be out of the way. Cobwebs around it told me that Hiram hadn't used it for some time. Shelves full of books were mounted on the walls here and there. Beside the stove hung several black cast iron fry pans. At one end of the camp, over Hiram's bed, was a deer head with the largest set of antlers I had ever seen. The camp seemed a part of Hiram.

"Only have sugar," he apologized. "Been out of Carnation for over a week." The end of March was a tough time. Supplies running low, ice too rotten to travel by the lake, and the haul roads were getting too soft to hold the sled's runners safely. As the days got longer, we were even more isolated until ice-out.

"Don't have any extra eggs," Hi said. "The girls won't be laying much until the sun gets stronger." His girls were hens. Ours were cows. Besides, there hadn't been a delivery of a case of eggs since October.

"That's Okay, I didn't come for eggs anyway."

"Good to have some company," Hi said. "What's on your mind?"

I didn't know how to start, so I just told him I was worried about what the future held for the King family. I didn't have to tell him why. Hiram knew what our family business was, just like the rest of the Village. Rum running was dangerous. Many lives had already been lost because of it. He seemed to nod his head just a bit.

"You say you want to know the future? Is that all?" He smiled a bit. I looked down at my cup and then back up.

"I don't know, maybe you could read coffee grounds or something." I was a little defensive, and probably sounded a bit rude. "Sorry," I said. "Didn't mean for it to come out like that."

Hi nodded and looked directly at me. I hated it when his eyes dug into mine that way. It was almost scary, like he had climbed in my head and wasn't going away until he was good and ready.

"There is a story about Wolverine who wanted to know what his future was. He asked the Wolf Spirit, 'What will be?' The Wolf Spirit looked at Wolverine and told him, 'There will be two paths ahead on your journey. One will be to the left, and one to the right. If you take the left one, you will live longer. If you take the right, you will die very soon, in moments.' Wolverine thanked the spirit and went on his way."

"Did he have to pay him?" I asked. I was thinking about palm readers I had read about in the daily *Bangor Whig and Courier*, "Know your future for only five cents," the ads read.

"No, there is never a payment to hear a spirit tell the future."

Hiram got up and stuffed another piece of white birch into the Atlantic Clarion box stove that was over-heating his cabin this warm afternoon. He had bread baking. The trade-off was a too warm cabin or no bread. It smelled so good. If the fire went out in the depths of winter, everything except the root cellar froze. Hi didn't go far during the winter months. There was no one else to keep the stove going.

"After Wolverine walked a while, he came to a place where the path split into two narrower ones, and he remembered what the spirit had said. Wolverine took the road to the left. Soon he came to a fast-flowing river. When he jumped in the river and began to swim across, the strong current flushed him down the rapids, and he drowned."

"But I thought he took the left path for a longer life?" I asked.

"He did. That was what the Wolf Spirit had told him. When Wolverine got to the forest in the sky, he went to find the Wolf Spirit. Wolverine asked him about his choice."

"'Why did you lie to me about the future?' Wolverine asked. The Wolf Spirit looked at him and said, 'I did not lie. If you had taken the other path, you would have been mauled to death by an angry catamount right away. By going left, you had a longer life before you quietly drowned.'"

Hiram stopped talking and looked out the window at a blue jay pecking at some suet he had been putting out for them all winter. The fat was in a little wire cage he made from chicken wire. Chickadees would land for a moment, but the blue jays dove at them, chasing the smaller birds away.

"It didn't matter, did it?" I asked.

"It's like what happens in the bull ring," Hi told me. I remembered seeing a picture of a matador in a history book when I was in school. "The matador is gored to death by the left horn or a few minutes later by the right horn; either way, the end is the same." After hearing about Wolverine, I wasn't sure that I wanted to know what was to come.

"See that canoe up there?" Hiram pointed to the green canvas canoe, a twenty foot White, hanging on ropes above us.

"What about it?" I asked.

"Notice the gash on the bow? It's on the other side." I got up, walked around so I could see the other side, a rip in the canvas, just at the water line, jagged pieces of the cedar frame poking through.

"What happened?" I asked.

"I made a decision about which route to take, but I didn't decide in time. Life flows ahead of us like a river," Hiram told me. "There are calm places to float through, and there are turbulent rapids to navigate safely. An experienced boatman can read the water, take the safest route around the rocks, paddle to the end of the rapids safely. If you come to a rock," he went on, "you have to decide to go to the left or the right. If you don't decide, the river does it for you, and you could wreck your canoe. Just like that one up there."

I wondered if Father had a difficult time with the decision to make moonshine. Most likely not.

Chapter 23

One morning in late April, Tommy, Louis and I walked with Father to check on the upper Boom House to see what they needed for supplies and to see how much pulp filled the double row of boom logs strung from pier to pier across the mouth of the West Branch. Louis needed to check on supplies for telephone line repairs he'd be making soon.

Boom logs were twenty-feet long and had a three-inch hole bored into each end. A heavy chain was threaded through the ends, connecting the logs together, making a huge necklace. Pulp wood floated down the rivers and filled the U-shaped string of boom logs. Once filled, the upstream end was connected together and the entire boom of logs and pulp wood floating inside it was towed from the river's mouth to Rip Dam. A second, empty string of logs was put in place to catch more wood floating down. After the boom reached the dam, the pulp was flushed down the river to the paper mill. The string of boom logs was towed back up the lake, and the process was repeated in a few days.

It was always good to know when a boom might be headed down the lake. Logs often slipped out, looking for a nice boat to crash into. The *Boom Jumper #2* was just pulling away from the dock as we arrived, on her way to round up some stray pulp wood that had escaped during the night. Father did his business, and we took one of the Company boats back, a low two board bateaux with a square stern for the silver Evinrude. Shuffling boats around was part of working for the Company. I looked around for the red-haired girl, but I didn't see her. Maybe next time, I hoped.

When we got back to the hotel, we were welcomed by the sweet smell of cedar burning in the kitchen stove, a kerosene lamp sputtering over the long table and the warm smell of freshly baked bread. Mother was just taking the loaves out of the oven. An uncut custard pie sat on the warming rack. A crock of baked beans with salt pork was in the oven. It was such a comfort to be in the kitchen with her. I was often reminded of the times she would have me on her lap and read to me, right here, in this kitchen and this rocking chair I'm sitting in now as I tell you this story.

Louis, Father and I pulled up to the table. It wasn't long before Uncle Amos arrived, hanging his derby on the coat hook. Tommy headed out to the barn to look after the horses. Father brought over three yellow enameled tin mugs, the ones with a green rim and ear. He poured a generous amount of Tanglefoot in each one. Tommy and I wouldn't ever get one of those, and I'm pretty sure that if offered, I'd say no. I've seen what drink can do to a man up here.

"That go-back road was a mean bitch this winter," Louis said. "Damned near lost the horse when she broke through the brush under the snow."

"Probably should have been sprinkled," Father said as he looked at me. "Remind me to have a chat with the walking boss about it next winter. Wouldn't do to lose a horse."

The walking boss was Jim Ross, a Westerner who came here to bring the drive into Bangor, no small feat in a drought year. Coordinating the pulses of water from pond to lake to river to pond again took some planning. There was just one chance to flush it all down river, or logs would be left high and dry and rotting. If that happened, no one got paid. The walking boss organized the winter cutting, laid out the haul roads, and chose the landings where the pulp was piled to wait for rising water in the spring.

Louis took another sip, then raised his glass to make a point. "This is really good, Caleb. Thought about aging it any?"

My stomach was starting to growl as I smelled the beans and stared at the pie.

"We filled ten oak barrels, and those are nearly a year old now. It's in your cup." Father poured him another while I dug into the custard pie Mother put in front of me.

When Mother left the kitchen, Father turned to Louis. "Amos and I have a little spying job for you." Father looked at Uncle Amos as if he hoped he would speak up. But he didn't say anything, just nodded a bit. Louis seemed to know a lot of folks in Bangor, and those contacts could be valuable.

Father outlined the job. "We want to find out who sabotaged the *Tethys*. Since you're familiar with the Nighthawk, you're the perfect choice. We think it may have been Fanny."

"I don't know, Caleb," Louis said. "Those people play rough and they play for keeps, if you know what I mean. It's pretty risky, and besides, that happened months ago. No one's going to be talking about it now."

"You'll be paid well," Uncle Amos said.

"Sure, but I can't spend the money if I'm dead now, can I?" Louis remarked.

"Would this put your mind at ease?" Father said, placing a pile of hundred-dollar bills on the table in front of him. Louis' eyes got pretty big. "If you're careful who you ask, there won't be a problem." I could see the money was tempting him.

Louis sighed. "You're making it pretty hard to refuse, Caleb. Okay, I'll see what I can find out on my next trip, but that won't be for a few more days."

"Maybe, but it needs to be as soon as the ice is out. We're going to Bangor the day the lake's clear. You come with us, but when we get there, we'll drop you off."

"What if someone sees us together?" Louis asked.

"They won't," Father replied. "We're dropping you off just before town, right near the seminary on the hill."

"Okay," Louis smiled. "Let's drink to tugging on the devil's tail!"

They shook hands and sealed the transaction with a toast, another refill, and one after that.

"Not used to this fine whiskey," Louis said as he stood, swayed once side to side, and then meandered toward the hall. "Think it's time to rest a bit," he slurred, his hand on anything nearby to steady his way up the narrow staircase, followed by a few chuckles.

After Louis left, Tommy came in from the barn. Mother had returned from upstairs and took the beans out of the oven. Fresh baked beans with salt pork, steaming slices of the bread I had been drooling over, and a tub of butter made a fine meal.

"What's this I heard about Louis doing something for you in Bangor?" Mother asked. She hadn't been on board with the 'shine business, but she went along since it was Father's idea.

"Oh, it's just finding out a little more about how much 'shine our buyer wants this season. It's too risky to have a big supply on hand. Then things get expensive if the law finds it." Father wasn't being honest with her, and I think she knew it by the expression on her face, something Father just ignored. Father seemed to create his own reality.

After we finished supper, Tommy and I cleared the table. Mother said something about finishing her sewing job and went upstairs while Tommy and I washed and dried.

Father was asking Uncle Amos about the stock we made this winter. "We have fifty cases and ten oak barrels," Uncle Amos reported. "The barrels are worth $7,500." Father seemed surprised, scrunching his brows. "The cases are all quarts, and at seven dollars per quart, the cases are worth $3,750. That's over ten grand for the whole lot," he continued. Uncle Amos was the math whiz of the family.

"I think we need to make one delivery for all of it," Father said. "Then we can continue with the weekly deliveries after that. We'll be out of room in the barn and storehouse at the Dam if we don't."

"Who has that kind of money?" Uncle Amos asked.

"Fanny might. We'll make a trip down river to set it up."

"Price the same as last year?"

Father thought a minute. "Seems fair to me. It's what she's been paying all along. She'll make a nice profit, and we can buy this hotel if we can convince the Company to sell it to us, and just maybe we can buy that potato farm in Aroostook County we talked about!" Things were certainly looking up for the King family.

"Charlie," Father called me back from the sink. "You and Tommy come over here."

"What is it?" I asked. Tommy had wiped his last dish and followed me over to the table.

"Be really alert about strangers poking around. You never know when the G-Men might get nosy or if there's someone else taking an interest in what we're doing in the barn." I don't think Father was as worried about the law as much as he was concerned about another explosion.

"Okay," I said. "I'll keep a careful watch." Tommy nodded in agreement, and we went back to finish the pots and pans.

All the whiskey stored in our barn was moved to the Dam in mid-March. Father was paying a retired dam tender to keep an eye on the shed where we stored it. We had made four trips with double sleds for the cases, but there was just one trip for the oak barrels. We finished moving everything down the lake just as the ice became too rotten to travel over, and we were marooned until spring break-up at the end of

April or early May.

I wondered about how we were able to make 'shine this long without getting caught. Once in a while the revenuers would sniff around the Dam. They rarely got to the Village. We knew people in the next county who had been busted, lost their farms, even went to prison, and Father reminded us constantly to keep a sharp eye out for strangers snooping around. Our problem was that there were three ways to come here, by boat from the Dam, the Deer Pond trace, and down the river in a canoe. We couldn't watch them all.

Chapter 24

The ice went out on May 8, 1921. The first day we could take a boat from our village cove all the way to the Company's pier at the Dam had been a topic of debate most of the winter. Ice would go early this year, frost was late. Or it would go out late because it was an open winter with little snow, making the ice six feet thick in places, five on the average. We could sometimes get an idea when this notable event would take place when we cut blocks for the ice house mid-winter.

An old privy was hauled out to the village cove, and a rope was tied to it with the other end through an iron ring set in the ledge on shore, a ring strong enough to hold back a five thousand cord boom. It would do for an outhouse. When the crapper fell through the ice, the person who registered the closest day and time won the pot, sometimes as big as $500.

As soon as the ice was clear of the cove and we could see an ice-free lake a few miles south, we got ready for the first trip of the season. The *Twilight* was slid off her winter's cradle and had been in the water for a few days while Father gave the engine a good going over. After a smooth ride down the lake, Father, Uncle Amos, Louis and I piled into the truck for a trip to Bangor. Louis and I were in the back, and it wasn't pleasant being tossed about. We had to see ahead to anticipate how to brace. It was exhausting.

We got to the seminary grounds late in the afternoon, as we had to ford two streams where bridges had washed away in the April rains and snow melt. We got stuck both times, having to use a block and tackle to pull ourselves out. Louis hopped out, and with his rucksack over his shoulder, headed in the direction of Union Street and Hammond, the same place we were going to. We couldn't be seen arriving together. Father knocked on the speakeasy's door. It opened after he gave his name, and we filed in behind him. We took seats at a round table in the corner. I sat between Uncle Amos and Father.

"Caleb," she greeted Father. We all stood. "It's really nice to see you. Oh please, sit. Did you have an easy trip? The roads must be quite soft still." Her perfume was nearly overpowering.

"We had a couple of challenges," Father said, "but nothing we couldn't handle." Uncle Amos was nodding his head in agreement. At that moment, Louis walked in, his small pack slung over his shoulder, and sat at the bar. He caught Father's eye. Instantly, Father looked back at Fanny.

"Everyone in Bangor heard about the boat fire last November. The spirits must have been looking out for you. What caused it?" she asked.

"There was a leaky fuel line in the engine area, and when the motor backfired, it set everything on fire. You're right, we were lucky to have survived." Father gave the appearance of being annoyed by the query when all the while he was getting over seeing Louis stroll in and sit at the bar just feet away. Fanny heard annoyance.

"Well, I'm glad you did. You people make the best 'shine in the state," and she smiled my way. "It would be a shame not to be able to offer Tanglefoot to my customers." It was all about business, I thought. It didn't seem to matter that seventeen men had died. Fanny hadn't been there to recover their bodies, lift them into the boat and cover them with a blanket. I thought Father was still wondering if she had been behind it. "What's on your mind to have come all the way down river to the big city?"

"We have cases of Tanglefoot plus some aged in oak casks. Our inventory has been building up all winter. I'd like to sell all of it. I think two big trucks would be needed."

Fanny and Father talked a little more, and soon the deal was done. We got all the supplies we needed after Fanny's men loaded twenty cases of empty Moxie bottles in the back of our truck. While we were in the Bangor Mercantile, I bought the new bike I had my eye on with the money I earned over the winter. It would fit nicely in the back of our truck, and I'd have to sit up front. Next, I'd buy the shotgun.

"It's good to have this settled," Father said.

"You seemed a bit surprised when Louis walked in," said Uncle Amos.

"Well, weren't you? I don't think she heard it in my voice, though."

"No, I don't think she did."

I kept watch in the rear-view mirror, but I didn't see any black wings following us home this time. We stayed in Dover that night.

After breakfast at the Blethen House the next day, we made our way back to the Grant Farm. We made a brief stop to make an extra deposit with the county sheriff and his deputy; Father wanted to be sure there would be no issues when making the delivery the next week.

Uncle Amos wasn't happy. "Don't you think that was too easy?" he asked Father.

"She knows a good deal when she sees one," he replied.

"A good deal for her, but in what way? We're putting the winter's work in a couple of trucks. It's an easy target. Besides, she isn't paying until it arrives."

"Amos, I'm just a good negotiator. It's that simple. And as far as collecting on delivery goes, she's been a loyal customer, and this is a big order." Uncle Amos just dropped his head, studying the floorboards of the truck. The topic seemed closed.

There was a crowd of river drivers waiting for us at the Grant Farm when we pulled in, some with spiked driving boots over their shoulders, sitting on benches on the covered porch that ran around three sides of the building. They were a rough looking bunch. "Bangor Tigers," we called them. They smelled a bit ripe, and in a few weeks, you'd want to be upwind and not too close. After a lunch, they piled into the back of the truck, and in a few more hours they would be safe in the hands of the Boom House clerk up the West Branch. The drive was about to begin as soon as the cold, spring rains raised the water levels in the ponds upstream.

I must have dozed off on the *Twilight*'s trip back to the village cove, but I woke up to hear Father raising his voice to Uncle Amos.

"We're doing this, Amos, whether you like it or not. I'm not going back on my word," he sputtered. "I don't like C.O.D. much myself, but I know she'll pay us like she promised." I knew Father was upset. It was rare that he was so angry that he sputtered. Uncle Amos sighed. He wasn't one to argue, and he didn't dare bring it up again.

The next day we were back at the Dam to load Fanny's trucks. Tommy had come along to help. Father had asked us to hitch a ride to the Grant Farm with Fanny's men so we could bring one of the Company's trucks back to the Dam. It had been stored there all winter. I'd learned how to drive the summer before, and I was excited to do this. It was nice to have Tommy along. It would take an hour to get there and another hour to return. Father had to make a short boat trip to a set of sporting camps on Ripogenus Lake, now part of our Chesuncook Lake, while we were gone. He assured us he'd be back in time to pick us up for the return trip to the Village. I was really looking forward to driving that truck all the way back to the Dam.

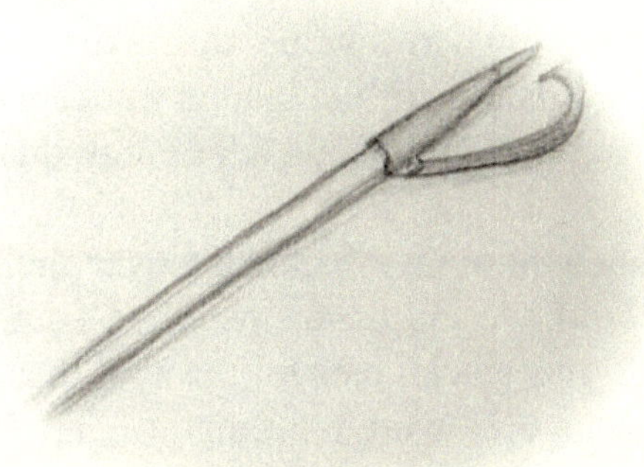

Chapter 25

Tommy and I squeezed in the back of one of Fanny's trucks. It wasn't the smoothest ride over recently thawed out roads. The surface was still a little soupy in places, but we were able to push through. It wasn't long before we got to the bottom of Sias Hill. There, we had to hook onto a cable that would winch us to the top. It was so steep, the trucks wouldn't have made it with the heavy loads in each one.

"Hook that around the frame, Tommy," I said. We had just walked up the hill and unreeled the winch's cable all the way down to the bottom. Once we hooked it onto the frame, we walked back up the hill to start the winch's engine and pull the truck to the top We brought the first truck up to the level area in front of the winch, and Tommy ran the cable back for the second one. After that truck reached the flat area at the top of the hill, we put the cable away and shut down the winch's motor.

The winch was set off into the woods a little as the road curved away at the top of the hill. The two trucks and their drivers waited for us beside the road about fifty feet away while we were finishing up. Using a hand crank, I reeled up the rest of the cable onto the drum.

"Help me with the canvas cover," Tommy said. I grabbed a corner and dragged the canvas over the machinery.

"Do I hear something coming?" Tommy asked. We looked up to see a truck arrive, dust billowing all around it. Because of the road's curve, the four men inside didn't see us at the winch which was somewhat hidden by brush.

We stayed put as the new arrival pulled over in front of Fanny's trucks waiting beside the road. "Let's watch from here and see what this is about." Tommy grabbed my arm and tugged me back to the cover of the bushes. I didn't understand why he wanted us to wait, but he seemed to know something I didn't. We squatted down to watch. Fanny's drivers were having a smoke while leaning against one of the loaded trucks we had just winched up the hill. The new arrival stopped just before it, dust swirling around.

"Four men are getting out, and they have bandanas over their faces," Tommy said. "I thought I could see the bandanas when I first saw the truck." Their derby hats and long black coats told us that these men were not woods workers. The guns they were pointing at Fanny's drivers told us we should stay hidden and still.

"Get your hands up," we heard one man with a sawed-off shotgun say. "Turn around and take off your shoes and socks," was the order. Fanny's drivers did as they were told without a word of protest. We kept quiet, too.

"Throw them into the cab," one man with a pistol said. Shoes and socks were thrown through the open window. "Put your hands behind your back." Another man pulled out a length of rope and tied their hands, walking them to the edge of the road and then lashing them to a tree.

"You're going to be sorry!" one of Fanny's drivers shouted out. A pistol slap across his face and a quick jab to his mid-section quieted him down. For a minute I thought they'd be murdered right there and then.

"Be really still," Tommy whispered. "We're dead if they see us." I nodded. If my fear were a scent, it would be nosed a mile away.

Two of the new arrivals holstered their pistols, jumped into Fanny's two trucks and drove away with the better part of our winter's production of 'shine. The remaining two climbed back into the truck they had arrived in and followed, clouds of dust everywhere for several minutes.

"Do you think it's safe to come out?" I asked Tommy.

"I don't think they have any reason to return," he answered. "Let's go." Tommy and I climbed out of the bushes.

"Hey, you two, come untie us!" one of Fanny's drivers yelled out. We ran over, freed them from the tree and got the ropes off their wrists.

"How'd you know to hide out?" the shorter one asked. I didn't like how he sounded, almost an accusatory tone to his words.

"Doesn't take a genius," Tommy said, "to know you need to be careful around these parts."

"You've got a smart mouth, kid," he said, and took a step toward Tommy, leaning a bit forward.

"Look, you're hauling ten grand of the devil's mouthwash. There's rarely any traffic on this road this early in the season, and neither one of you seem armed. Besides, I saw them with their faces covered when their truck came around the corner right in front of us." Tommy held his ground and the driver backed off.

"What's your shoe size?" the other driver asked us.

"Too large for you guys," Tommy said, recognizing they had an eye on our foot gear.

"We'll get you something," I said. I walked back to the woods and gathered some birch bark. It wasn't long before I fashioned two pair of sandals using some black spruce roots for string.

"It's a few miles to the Grant Farm," I said. "We'd better get going. It's doubtful there'll be someone along to give us a ride anytime soon." The four of us started walking. The sandals I made stood up pretty well; I had to re-string them only once.

"Say, these work great," one driver said. "But I don't think they'll wear very well."

"We only care about the next few miles," I said.

When we made it to the Grant Farm, I called the Boom House at the Dam. The clerk answered. I was hoping that Father had returned from his trip to the sporting camps on Ripogenus.

"It's Charlie King," I said. "Can you get my Father to the phone right away?"

It took a moment. I wasn't looking forward to this conversation.

"Charlie? What's wrong?" Father asked.

"We were hijacked by four men with guns," I told him. "Both trucks are gone."

"What?" He shouted.

"Four guys with guns held us up at Sias Hill after we had finished winching the trucks to the top." I knew he had heard me but wasn't believing his ears.

"Everything is gone?" Father asked.

"Yes," I said. "Everything's gone."

"Is anyone hurt? Are you two okay?" He asked. I thought about what he asked for first, but I wasn't surprised that he seemed more concerned about the missing 'shine.

"No, just that Fanny's drivers have some sore feet," I reported.

"What?" He asked. I didn't try to explain.

"Do we still shuttle the Company truck back to the Dam?" I asked, ignoring his question. "And what about Fanny's two drivers?" I didn't mention they'd need shoes as the supply room at the farm would have a size to fit them. Besides, there'd be too much explaining.

"There's a truck here that I can borrow. I need to ask those two drivers a few questions. I'll come for you. See if you can find out if they can hitch a ride down river later today after I've talked with them."

"Okay," I said, "and if there's no one?"

"They may want to call Bangor, but warn them not to give any details over the phone. Folks listen in. Maybe Fanny can send someone up to fetch them." Father hung up. It'd be an hour before he got here, so Tommy, the two drivers and I had an early supper. We were hungry from the walk and tired out, too.

By the time Father arrived, Fanny's drivers had already hitched a ride to Lily Bay with the mail truck. There, they'd board the steamer for Greenville Junction where they'd get on a train that would take them back to Bangor. Father wasn't happy to have missed them. Now he had no one to cross-examine except me and Tommy.

"And you hid in the bushes?" he asked after we got in the cab.

"We were just putting the winch away, so it was good timing," Tommy explained. "They would have seen us pulling the cable across the road if they had pulled in ten minutes earlier. We were lucky. I'm surprised they left the two drivers as witnesses. They might not have left four."

It was Tommy's experience hanging out in the London Dockland that gave him the caution he showed at Sias Hill. It was a good thing Tommy saw them wearing bandanas. Things might have been very different had he not been with me.

While we walked to the boat, Father said, "Boys, I don't want you to talk about what happened with anyone except me, Louis and Amos. Be sure you mention nothing about it to Mother. I don't want her to worry."

"Okay," we said at the same time. Tommy and I cast off the lines while Father started the motor. We didn't talk much on the ride back to the Village. I could see Father's jaw clenching and relaxing, the stub of a soggy cigar moving from one side of his mouth to the other. Soon we were back on the *Twilight* and headed up the lake. At least we had the supplies we needed to continue running the stills.

Father and Uncle Amos were sitting at the kitchen table the next morning when Louis came in from the porch and joined them. Tommy and I were filling the wood box.

"I should have listened to you, Amos" Father told him. "You were right."

"Doesn't matter who's right or wrong. We need to find out what happened. Maybe Louis will get back soon with some news."

The days passed. I worked the still the way Uncle Amos taught me. He was looking for the moose we'd often see munching lily pads at the north end of the island. He wouldn't be back for a few more days. We had to rebuild our stock, so the still had to run all day and all night. Sometimes Tommy took a break from the barn chores and the horse shoeing to give me a hand. Mother brought us lunch, sometimes supper, too. The three stills kept me pretty busy, and I was glad when Uncle Amos came back a little early with a nice moose hide and meat in his canoe. While waiting for the boiler to heat up, Uncle Amos and Tommy would re-shoe some of the 300 horses the Company kept in the field in back of the barn. We kept busy.

Not long after the hijacking, I had another dream about the black wings, coming towards me, fading back, surging ahead like they were sliding back and forth on a wire. Then I was in the barn. Something was sitting on the cross beam near the entry door I had just stepped through. It was turning its head toward me. I couldn't make out any kind of face, but I knew somehow it had one. Eyes opened in the darkness, glowing with fire, looking right at me. When I woke up, I was nearly out of breath. The dream faded, I calmed, and I fell into a dreamless sleep until dawn. I needed to talk with Hi.

Chapter 26

Mother needed more eggs than our hens were laying, so off I went to Hiram's to see what he could sell us. I could see spring coming on my way up the path to his cabin. The berry bushes were all blossomed, and the apple trees showed signs of a good crop.

"Hello the camp," I shouted as soon as I saw it. Hiram was on the roof, sliding a piece of flat driftwood under some cedar shingles to help shed the rain.

"I'll be down soon, one way or the other," he said as he stepped down the rickety ladder, black spruce roots tying the pine rungs to the rails, groaning with every step.

"How many?" he asked.

"Many what?"

He sighed, "I can see the basket under your arm, Charlie. Or are you here for another reason and just like to carry around an empty egg box for fun?"

"Oh," I said. "Mother would like to know if you could give us two dozen?"

"Let's see what's out there." Hi motioned for me to come around the side of the cabin and through the chicken wire screen door. We went from the main pen to the laying boxes, set high on stilts to discourage the foxes and martins, roofed over with cooling cedar bark like the clapboards on the back side of the hotel.

We picked up two dozen for Mother, and Hi took a few back to the cabin for cooking later on. He beckoned me on, and I followed him inside. I wanted to ask about that awful dream.

He looked at me, not making a sound or gesture, just digging into my eyes again with his.

"Did your mother ever tell you about her grandfather?" Hi kept his gaze.

"A while ago, I think. Why?"

"What do you remember?" Hi asked. I didn't know what he was thinking, but that wasn't unusual for a chat with Hiram.

"Mother said something about her Grandfather Neptune, a Penobscot Chief in Old Town or Orono. Don't remember which."

It was at that moment that I realized I was part Penobscot Indian. Would that explain….no, not possible I thought, although my hair was black and straight, and I had high cheekbones and brown eyes.

"Chief Neptune was the most powerful chief of all." Hiram paused. "I know I'm not a Penobscot, but a Mic-Mac, different tribe entirely. I do know about other tribes, though, especially in the case of Chief Neptune. He was a powerful shaman and well known throughout the Nation."

"What's a shaman?" I had no idea about the culture at all. You might think that odd, living around, working with and sometimes playing with many different tribes as they came and went through the seasons. The Penobscots gathered at the mouth of Caucmagomic every August when the fishing and berry picking were the best. When the Company wanted to make it easier to pull a boom through the mouth of the river, the sand bar at the river's mouth was bulldozed down, ruining the fishing and the tribe's annual potlatch but making more money for the Company's investors. The Penobscots never returned to their sacred gathering place.

"A shaman is a powerful leader, someone who has magic powers. All the Neptunes had powers. Some could summon the winds, the thunder, the caribou or the rains." Hiram waved his hand in front of the window, gesturing to the outside world.

"You've seen the black wings, Charlie King who is a Neptune, something lurking in the shadows, and now another dream is my guess?"

Speechless, I turned to look out the window. Forget-Me-Nots were getting ready to bloom. Some shoots of bamboo were showing. I could see Mother cooking these along with a mess of fiddleheads. They all seemed to arrive out of the ground at the same time in May. The brief vision faded. Did I have bad dreams and see things in the dark, things that weren't really there because I had some power I had not known about?

"I've had some strange dreams," I said. "Scary mostly. Same

dream, someone or thing sitting on a rafter in the barn. It looks at me with fire in its eyes."

"That is a spirit dream. The meaning will be clear; sometimes it takes a while." Hiram looked away a moment. "Have you had another experience with the south wind like you told me about?"

"No, nothing more. Just some bad dreams," I replied. We talked more about dreams, and then Hiram had to get back to work.

Hi got up. "You should go, young Neptune. I have more work to do on this roof before it rains tonight."

I shut the door, hopped down the three hand-split wooden steps, and delivered the eggs just in time so Mother could make bread. Uncle Amos had been looking for me, she said. He needed me to help with the bottling.

Chapter 27

With Tommy's help, the batch was all bottled up after lunch. Sun streamed in through the strip of windows above the horse stalls and through the open barn doors. Soon, we had twenty cases ready to ship. Father and Uncle Amos were making some minor adjustments to some of the equipment when I saw Louis ride into the yard. We heard him shout for us and walked outside. Finally, he returned. We were getting a little worried.

Louis was on horseback, a pretty girl sitting behind him in the saddle, holding the reins of another horse toting some bed rolls and saddle bags.

"This is Anna," Louis nodded towards the girl hanging on to him. "I should say, meet Mrs. Maki." She smiled. There was a thin silver ring on her finger. "We got married yesterday," Louis announced. Anna smiled at us, contentment showing on her face, her cheek against his shoulder. She was pretty, thin, and wearing way too much rouge and lipstick for the Village. She seemed a little shy for one of Fanny's girls. I later learned that she first arrived in Bangor the same afternoon Louis did.

"If you listen real careful like, you'll be able to hear Fanny swearing all the way from Bangor," Father crowed, shaking his head with a grin on his face. Louis had run off with and married one of Fanny's girls.

"Hope Fanny won't be swearin' at us," I heard Uncle Amos say.

"I hope to Christ you kept your head down," Father barked at Louis. "Does Fanny know you live up here?

"Nope, still doesn't." Louis looked over his shoulder, smiling at

Anna. He wasn't convincing.

No one spoke. Louis waited a moment. He climbed off the horse, turned and offered a hand to Anna who slid off the saddle to the ground. Louis checked the bed roll lashings. "Anna has something to tell you about Fanny."

Anna looked at Louis. "It's okay, Anna. These are friends. Tell them what you told me at the Nighthawk."

She waited a moment, stared at her feet as if she were unsure if she should share what she knew. "It was Fanny who took her own shipment. She wanted it to look like a hijacking."

"How do you know?" Father asked, doubt showing clearly on his face.

"I was having a drink at the Nighthawk with this guy from Boston a while back." Anna flung back her hair. She had Father's attention at 'Boston.' "He was joking about how Fanny had stolen her own whiskey, so she wouldn't have to pay for it, and blamed the loss on some gang from Boston. Said she was pretty clever."

Father's jaw seemed locked in place. His face was slowly reddening, showing his anger.

"Are you sure about that?" Uncle Amos asked. "You couldn't have misunderstood?"

"He was pretty clear about it. He even went on to say how stupid anyone would be to trust her so much." At this, she shrunk back a bit, as if she were unsure of how Father would react.

Father looked at her while she spoke, deciding whether to believe her or not. I could tell the moment he accepted what she said. It was when he heard the word, 'stupid.' Father thanked her, grabbed Uncle Amos' arm and walked away to the barn.

"That might be right, Caleb, and that was a lot of money we lost," Uncle Amos said. "But remember what I said about getting revenge. We have to be sure."

"Didn't lose the money, Amos. We just never got it. She bought that shipment from us, and she's going to pay one way or another." Father had his own way of looking at things.

Louis was already back on the horse and reached his hand to Anna. She hopped up behind him as nimble as a cricket. Father and Uncle Amos turned and waved.

"We'll be at my camp." Louis tugged gently on the reins, turning his horse away. The second horse with all of their luggage tied on followed behind, its reins in Anna's hand. We stared as they rode off. I couldn't help but imagine a pretty red-haired girl sitting behind me as we rode off together.

I went back to the barn where Uncle Amos had been making drift pins for a new pier. I worked the bellows on the coal fire, making the steel red and then white again as he pounded away. Uncle Amos came back in, tied up his leather apron, got on his forge gloves and glasses. Then he grabbed the tongs and took a piece of round iron from the coals.

"What now?" Uncle Amos asked after hammering a point on a white-hot spike.

"I think we should give Fanny a little present," Father said, the stub of a well chewed cigar wiggling in his mouth like a worm. Mother called for dinner, and we all headed into the house.

Warm rolls were on the table along with some venison, baked potato and greens. Father and Uncle Amos talked about the plan a little after Mother went to her quilting bee. There would be a nice wedding ring quilt for Anna and Louis in a few weeks. And the rocking chair I'm sitting in right now? Mother let Louis and Anna borrow it to get their new arrival to sleep. Anna was expecting in early spring. I brought it over the next day.

Father and Uncle Amos came up with a plan for revenge. It involved recruiting the county sheriff who happened to be on our payroll, not hers. If that plan went as expected, we'd surely hear Fanny swearing all the way from down river.

That evening, Father let Fanny know there was another shipment coming, same time the next week. This time the terms were different. She would have to send the trucks and the cash. She agreed, but she complained about having lost her trucks the last time. She'd have to find replacements. Nothing was said about payment for the lost shipment, and nothing was said about Anna or Louis. I overheard Father tell Uncle Amos that we were in the clear for now, but we might not be for long.

My orders were to fill all but five cases of Moxie with water. Then, I was to fill eight oak barrels with water, too. The total load would be the same as last time. The difference was that the County Sheriff would be waiting for her drivers at the Nighthawk when the trucks arrived to unload in the back alley. The real stuff was in front, the water filled bottles and barrels were in the back of the load. Father always gave a few bottles to the drivers to keep them happy. The law would take the cases and barrels in front for themselves. Fanny would lose her trucks, we'd have her cash, her men would be arrested, and the Nighthawk would be trashed. Maybe she'd get arrested, too. We wouldn't be out much and would recover some of what we lost. It was the hardest punch Father could have thrown. It wouldn't be safe to deal with Fanny any longer. He was going to have to find another buyer if we were going to stay in the business.

Chapter 28

A week passed. The cool mornings gave way to black flies and some heat by noon. A good breeze was needed to be able to work outside without a bug hat. I was glad I didn't have to work in the garden anymore that afternoon. The peas were all planted.

It was later in the afternoon when Father found me cleaning up at the kitchen sink. "Charlie, you and Tommy take the canoe up river to the Depot at the bend. Black Sebat ordered a case to celebrate the end of the drive when it comes in. It's late in the afternoon, so while you're up there, see if you can get some perch for supper," Father suggested. Black Sebat was Sabattus Mitchell, a St. Francis chieftain. His tribal home was on the St. Francis river near Quebec. He was a large man and had the strongest grip of anyone I had shaken hands with, like putting yourself into a vice. He ran the drive when Jim Ross was busy elsewhere, a substitute walking boss.

"Okay," I said, and went to look for Tommy. He was helping Uncle Amos shoe one of the oxen. I was glad to have a break from the Moxie that wasn't.

We loaded a case into the canoe and threw in our fishing poles, worm can and fish pail. The perch had just started to bite, and we loved a fish fry. We might have a mess tonight, I hoped. And I hoped for one more thing: to see a young lady with red hair.

We took the square stern Old Town canoe with the 5hp Neptune. There was that word again, I thought, as I wrapped the pull cord twice around the flywheel. Neptune was a god of the sea. I remembered that when we had studied mythology. I wondered how it came to be the name of a famous Indian shaman.

We had just pulled out of the cove when the wind picked up, making us go way around Goose Grass Flats to keep from getting soaked from the spray as we hit the waves. Rounding the corner, we could see the two piers with triple strings of boom logs across the river. These long logs held back nearly five thousand cords of pulp wood that had been driven down the river to this collection point. The Boom House was coming up on our left, so I cut the motor back, and we drifted along the side of the pier where the steel *Boom Jumper* was tied up. Tommy jumped out to hold us back just before we hit the clay bank. I was coming in too fast.

"In a rush, are you?" he shouted at me, pushing back at the canoe that nearly knocked him over; I pretended to be busy with the motor while looking around for that red-haired girl.

"Let's go," I said, and walked through to the bow and stepped out. "Better not forget this." I grabbed the case of Tanglefoot that had been Tommy's seat on the way up and followed him to the clerk's camp. All the men were on the drive at Pine Stream Falls, or they were on the boats with the last boom being hauled down the lake to the Dam. No one would be around except the cook, and he was probably napping after making donuts for the men at three that the morning.

Sabat met us on his porch. He pointed to the floor where we were to put the wooden case, nodded his head, and went back in the camp.

"Doesn't say much, does he?" I remarked on the way back to the canoe.

"Not many of them seem to. They've been taken advantage of just like me and my brother were. There's anger underneath their calm faces; I can feel it," Tommy said.

We were almost back to the canoe when we heard, "Hey, you two." We turned to look, and there she was, Abby Ross, hair as red as fire, Stetson hat, in pants.

"What?" I said.

"I've got to get out of here." She came closer. "I'm going out of my mind in this place, looking at tally slips all day. Think you could take me fishin'? I hear the perch are starting to bite two bends up Pine Stream." She looked at me and smiled. I forgot all about the night she nearly killed us and the horses pulling the sprinkler.

"Grab your stuff. That's where we're heading, but bring your own worms and bucket." She was so pretty; I wondered that I could say anything.

She ran up to her cabin for her gear. This was better than I could have imagined.

Abby found her way to the middle seat of the canoe after I climbed in, then Tommy pushed us out, planting himself on the front seat. I started the motor, and we picked our way up river around floating pulp wood to Pine Stream. As we turned away from the West Branch into the little stream, we saw a canoe with two men paddling down river, dodging the pulp wood floating down to the boom. They didn't look like river men, and I wondered if the Thoreau seekers were starting early this season.

Right after I dropped the anchor, we were pulling in white perch one after the other, big ones, too. We had a bucket of forty when we decided we had better quit. Abby had ten in hers.

We planned to do it again soon if we could get away, and we left Abby at the dock with her catch. Tommy and I headed back to the hotel with supper. After we put the canoe away, we had to fillet and skin.

Somehow, I felt different. I couldn't wait to see Abby again. I'd find a way to get back in a day or two.

"Who's that coming up the lane?" I asked Mother as I set the bucket of perch fillets in the sink. Outside were the two men we had seen up river. With their wide brimmed hats, the men looked like they had been traveling more than a couple of days. They asked if they could stay a night, have supper and breakfast and a packed lunch for the next day.

The two men didn't say much and they didn't mingle with the other guests. It was after breakfast when we learned who they really were. After she packed their lunches, Mother went upstairs to clean rooms. Tommy and I had finished dishes, and Tommy was headed down the hallway on his way out to the barn to heat up the forge while I fussed with an old boot lace before I joined him. Uncle Amos and Father were sitting at the ends of the kitchen table when the two men came in and sat down between them on the side. One was short and one had a hooked nose. They smiled, and each placed a pistol on the table, their hands on the grips. Father and Uncle Amos froze. Father stared at them.

"What do you want?" Father asked.

"We have a proposition," the shorter man said. "You, the producer, are going to supply us, the new customer, every drop of 'shine you can make."

"Why the guns?" Uncle Amos asked.

The shorter man continued, "It's to impress upon you the necessity of making the same excellent 'shine you did for Fanny. The difference is that you'll be making it for us."

"We're not in that business anymore," Father lied.

"You've had a little vacation, we'd call it. Now you're back to work. In a week, you are to make this delivery to the Dam." He handed Father a scrap of paper. "And on the back is how much you will receive for your effort. Any less effort, well, we'll just say we know where you live and who lives with you. Let's see, there's your lovely wife, Grace, for starters. We understand you're away from home during the daytime, and sometimes overnight. This is a rough part of the country," he continued. "It would be a shame if anything bad happened to your family."

"That's right," the other said. "And it would be too bad if anymore of your shipments to Bangor disappeared."

Father's expression changed slightly, but it was Uncle Amos who showed he understood what was not said. It wasn't Fanny who had hijacked her own load to avoid paying. The Boston crew had done it, just as Uncle Amos had suggested. If Father didn't get it then, he did now. And it put the boat explosion on their doorstep, too. Boston had been trying to shut Fanny down, and we had just done it for them. You'd think they'd be grateful.

Father looked at them a moment. I couldn't tell what he was thinking. He turned over the paper, noting the figure written on the back. "It's half of what the shipment is worth."

"You can understand," the man with the hook nose spoke, "that the value is exactly what Mr. Smith says it is." He moved his pistol a little to make the point, and then he turned to his partner. "Markets aren't what they used to be, are they Mr. Wesson?" The other man shook his head.

"Markets change all the time," Mr. Wesson agreed.

"Then we understand one another," the shorter man said to Father. "You'll be paid on delivery at the Dam every Thursday. And don't bring your sheriff friend. That wouldn't be appreciated. Like I said, we know where you live and who lives here with you. Now be sure to enjoy the rest of your day."

The two thugs got up, put the guns away, and walked out the door, boxed lunches in hand. When they got in the canoe and began paddling down the lake, Father finally spoke.

"I didn't think this business could become such a problem. Did you, Amos?" "No. Do we go along?"

"No. And I don't like how they've threatened our family."

"So, we're not making the delivery to the Boston guys? I didn't like those threats much," Uncle Amos said.

"Those bastards," Father said. "Besides paying only half price, they blew up my boat! There's no way I'm giving them anything! I have plans for them. They'll get the same that Fanny did."

"Better act fast, Caleb," Uncle Amos said. "Those guys won't wait long before they pay us another visit, and I don't think we'd enjoy their company as much, do you? I sure don't want to be dancing on the Devil's tail."

"You're right, Amos," Father said. "Set up the load like we did for Fanny. I'll send Louis ahead to let the sheriff know when, what and where. Before they load, Louis will have to take the truck at the Dam and head out with the description the deputies will need to make the stop."

"Think that'll do it?" Uncle Amos asked.

"I don't see why not. It'll teach them not to mess with folks up here." Father was clenching and releasing his fists. He was pretty mad. I hadn't seen him do that before. It wasn't any fun to be around him when he was becoming angry. I wanted to go fishing again and asked. Father just nodded his head, and I ran for my boots before he could change his mind.

"Better watch your blood pressure," Uncle Amos said.

"To Hell with my blood pressure," Father sputtered, his voice getting louder. "Don't you have some work to do in the barn?" Uncle Amos knew better than to push anymore, and he grabbed his hat, heading for the forge where Tommy was waiting for him.

Chapter 29

A few mornings later, when I got my chores done early, Father let me go fishing again, mostly because he needed someone to go to the Boom House and tow back a boat one of the river drivers had used and left there. Tommy was busy helping Amos and couldn't come. I think Father was glad to have me out of the way while he was thinking about his latest problem. It seemed the more he thought about things, the angrier he got. I hopped into the canoe, nearly forgetting the bait can and fish bucket, fired up the outboard and scooted up the lake to the Boom House before he could change his mind. I was glad to get away from his growing bad mood.

There she was, sitting at the end of the float on an empty wooden crate with a sarsaparilla label on the side, line in the water, hanging from a thin alder pole. I pulled in a little slower than last time. Abby grabbed the side of my canoe as it was about to scrape the edge of the float.

"Hey, want to go up river and see if the fish are biting?" I asked her as I drifted to the dock.

"I was hoping someone would come rescue me," she said as she smiled. "because they sure aren't biting here. I'm ready. Just have to load this gear into the canoe."

When we got to the bend of Pine Stream, I released the anchor, using a little rope that ran through pulleys from my stern seat to the bow. With the canoe anchored off its bow, it would swing in the current, and we wouldn't be caught sideways if any pulp wood drifted our way.

We sat forever, I felt, not saying a word. The sun was warm on our faces, and the smell of sun-warmed pine pitch drifted through the forest on some late morning mist. "I hope we catch something," I finally said. We hadn't had a nibble.

"Me, too," she said, " but if we don't, we can always come back and try again." We stayed at the bend of the stream for another half hour.

"Maybe they'll be biting now back at the Boom House," she offered. I agreed. It was around lunch time, and the cook would have thrown the garbage off the dock by the time we got back.

I pulled the anchor, started up the motor, and we went back to the dock. This time, we shared the sarsaparilla box, our feet dangling in the water. Then the fish started to bite. We were busy reeling them in, throwing them back or in the bucket, baiting the hook again and throwing out the line over and over.

"I got another one," she cried out, "and this one is really big." The tip of her pole bent nearly in half as she reeled it in. The fish fought her all the way. When it was just below the surface, we could see it was a huge salmon, at least five pounds. Its silvery scales glistened colors in the bright sun, dark spots all along the upper half of its body.

"Quick, get it in the bucket before it spits out the hook," I said. We both had a grip on it and were able to drop it into the pail. Our hands were beside each other when they touched. I turned to her with a smile. I almost forgot about the salmon. Abby squeezed my hand, and then our eyes met. She smiled back, the warm sun bathing our faces.

"The last one I caught wriggled back into the ice hole. It was almost as big," I said. I wanted to tell her about the wind I had summoned, but she wouldn't have believed me, I thought.

"We'll have it for supper tonight," Abby offered.

"Why don't we fish a little more and then you can come back to the hotel with me. Mother does a nice job with salmon, and I know she'd like to meet you."

"If she won't mind an extra person at the table, let's see if we can get some perch to go along with it," she agreed, and smiled at me again. "It's been a lot of fun fishing with you, Charlie," she said.

"Me too," I replied. I was feeling a little warm in the face like that time at the Nighthawk. Abby was really special, and I was glad she liked me. I had never felt this way before. I think I had fallen in love.

After we got back to the village cove, we filleted and skinned the fish at the dock, dumping the remains at the lake shore for the coons, eagles and ospreys, and now we needed to wash up. As Abby and I walked back to the hotel, the wind had come up a little.

"My father used to tell me stories about a shaman who could summon the wind," she said, lifting her collar against the cool breeze.

"Only when he was angry, right?" I asked. She stopped in the middle of the road.

"How did you know? Have you heard the same tale?" she asked.

"Mother told me about it," I fibbed. I really wanted to tell Abby about my own experiences. Then, I decided to take a chance, hoping she wouldn't laugh at me.

"Remember I told you about the salmon I lost through the ice hole last winter?"

"Yes, and sometimes they do get away," she said.

"I got pretty steamed up about it."

"I can imagine," she said. "Wasn't the same salmon we caught today, right?"

"No," I laughed, "but there's something more."

"What's that?" she asked.

"About the wind," I answered. "After the salmon got away, I got really mad, and the wind came up strong and fast. It blew me over the clear ice right to shore." Abby's expression changed. She wasn't smiling anymore.

"You're not going to tell me that the wind came up because you were angry, are you?"

"Your father's story about summoning the wind might be true," I said. I could see Abby was thinking about what I said.

"Do you have any Indian blood, Charlie?" Abby asked.

"On Mother's side."

"Well, it's not the craziest thing I've ever heard," she commented. "Are you really sure about it?"

"Pretty sure, but I don't get angry very often," I said. "The south wind doesn't turn the lake into whitecaps because I feel like it."

"Well, let me know when it's about to happen again so I can tie myself to a tree or something. Wouldn't want to blow away," and she smiled at me again.

"Okay, I'll let you know," I said. And that was it. I had shared a deep and fantastic secret and felt so relieved. "Do you have grandparents?" I wondered.

"My Grandmother Molly lives in Nicatou," she said. "She's a shaman in her village."

"It would be nice to meet her," I said.

"I'm hoping my father will take me to see her. It's been too long."

When we got to the kitchen, I introduced Abby to Mother. The perch and the salmon were put away in the ice box. Mother asked Abby questions about her family and what she liked to do. Mother was really interested in Abby. So was I. I could hear Father calling me from the barn.

"Go see what he wants, Charlie," Mother said to me. "Abby and I have more to talk about."

When I got to the barn, Father was looking over a ledger of accounts. His jaw-clenching anger from the morning had turned into a full blown rage. Amos and Tommy were outside by the pig sty.

He was pretty hot. "Do you understand what those men want from us?" If a cigar had been in his mouth, he would have bitten it in two.

"I think I do," I said. "If we cooperate, we get half of what Fanny was paying."

Father stormed some more, throwing a coffee mug across the room, smashing it against the stall door. When his anger boiled over like this, there wasn't anything to be said that would calm him down. As Father cleaned up the broken pieces of coffee cup, the redness left his face. "You have to understand how serious this is."

"Okay," I said. "What if those guys don't get back?" I asked him. To this day I have no idea where that thought came from. "That would send a message, wouldn't it? Do we have anything to lose, really?"

Father just looked at me. Those were more words than I had said to him at once for a very, very long time. They must have been the right ones, though. What I was suggesting came from a place inside my soul that I wanted to lock away.

"Maybe I can take the boat out this afternoon," he said with a little smile. "See where they are. It's a long paddle to the next campsite, and they're probably still on the lake. Maybe they need help with their canoe or something." Mother was calling us for supper. Father walked back to the house while I closed the barn doors.

Because the men had guns, any plans to deal with them were risky. I didn't want to see my family hurt. The business had caused some trouble, but we were on our way to owning the hotel and the potato farm in the County. I had my new bike, and the shotgun I had ordered the last trip down river would be here in a few more days. I felt something stirring inside, an anger bubbling to the surface. There was a tingling on the back of my neck, and it crept up my scalp. I was angry about the threats to our family, angry about losing my brothers, angry at the government. I could hear the wind was rising from the south end of the lake. Soon, the lake's surface was covered in white capped waves, swells growing as my anger increased, and soon the foam on the wave tops was being torn off the peaks. First there'd be white, then a cloud of spray. Waves crashed on the ledges on Gero, sending plumes of spray nearly to the tree tops.

Father called from the house. "Charlie, bring in Duke from the pasture. There's a big storm comin' in."

The wind, now a gale, wouldn't quiet down, and I was still pretty angry. I went to the barn and buttoned it up. I got Duke into his stable. He was eager to go inside, but shied away from me as I reached for his halter. It took three tries to hold on to him.

As I came into the kitchen, my parents were busy closing windows. Abby was at the counter. She had been helping Mother prepare the salmon for the oven.

"Where'd that wind storm come from, Charlie?" she asked. "There's hardly a cloud in the sky."

"Hard to say," I replied. "We probably just missed seeing it come up the lake." Now that was a lame explanation. If anything, all of us 'Suncookers could read the sky and predict the weather.

"Help me with these dishes?" Abby asked me.

"Sure," I said, and I walked over to dry.

"You seem a little tense," she said. "I'd guess a bit angry? Something happened in the barn?"

"Enough to get me riled up a little," I said.

"You know, the wind can come up fast, but it can be a while before it calms down. Sometimes I used to rub my dad's temples when he was upset. Can I do that for you?" She was already drying off her hands, anticipating my saying 'yes.'

The howling increased. In my anger I had summoned the spirit of the south wind, and it showed no sign of letting up. The waves built so high they crashed over the breakwater along the shore. The giant pine that had been on the point forever snapped off twenty feet up the trunk, exposing a rotten core surrounded by a pristine shell.

"Okay," I said. Abby stood behind me, and with her fingers on my temples, gently massaged the tension away. The wind calmed down as she did.

"Might be a good idea to get a handle on your temper," she said. "Wouldn't want the barn roof to blow off." It was an hour before the lake calmed completely.

After supper, Tommy and Uncle Amos had a little more work to do in the barn, so they headed outside.

"Charlie, saddle up a horse and get Abby home before it storms again. I don't like the looks of that sky," Mother said. We saddled up Duke, who was glad for some attention, and I brought Abby back to the Boom House.

The next day we learned that two bodies had washed up on shore at Sandy Point, and that an overturned canoe with some camping gear lashed inside was found not far away. I prayed we wouldn't be getting a visit from Mr. Springfield and Mr. Colt.

It wasn't long before I used my power again.

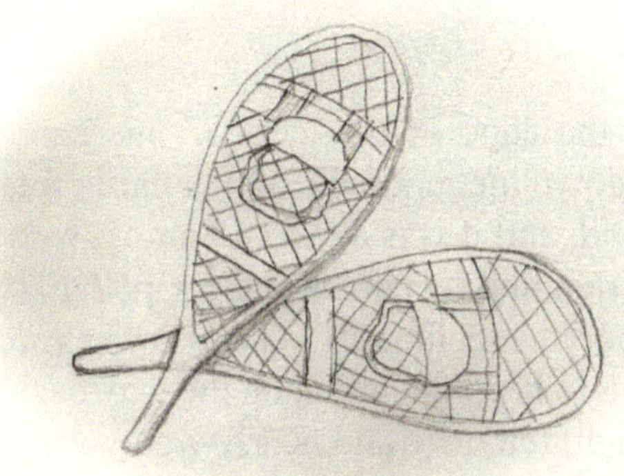

Chapter 30

It was time for another trip to Hiram's. He was weeding his corn, beans and squash wrapped around the tall stalks, the old way of planting.

"That Southie the other day," Hiram said, "came out of nowhere."

"I know," I said. "I got really angry."

"Then you have found your power," he said, "and from now on, any indignity can be met. You are a Neptune, and you are a shaman." Hiram bowed a bit from his waist, holding it a moment. I told him the same story I told Abby, of the lost salmon and my anger as I was blown to shore over the clear ice. Hiram wasn't surprised. It was like he knew I could summon the wind before I did!

"I came to ask you something," I said. "I don't need eggs, not today, anyhow."

"Come," Hi said. "Let's have some tea." We went inside.

I told Hiram about the men with pistols who had threatened us. Had I not asked the wind spirits to help, I was afraid that Father would have run them down in his boat.

"You used your power wisely, Charlie of the Neptunes. It was a hard decision but the right one to protect your family."

"Did you ever have to make a decision like that?" I asked.

"Not the same situation, but I have had to protect myself," Hi said. "One day I climbed above the tree line and met Pamola. It took me most of the morning to climb up there. I wrapped my sacred blanket around my shoulders more for its power and protection than for its warmth."

"Did you see him?"

"Not at first. Once I thought I saw some black wings circling around the peaks. I learned later that the spirit of the Nighthawk also lived there."

"Did you get close?"

"As close as those trees at the edge of the garden," his hand waved to his yard. "Lightning flew down the mountain at me, hard rain, hail, and a foot of snow. I was so cold, and it was all from Pamola who wanted to keep me away from his den and to punish me for being so stupid to climb up above the tree line. I had a flask of ockoby, what you call "whiskey," and I drank most of it to keep me going on the way back down. I couldn't get down fast enough, fell once and nearly went over a huge cliff. I didn't have much power then."

"What power did you have?" I asked.

"I was able to summon the eagle and osprey who would defend me from my enemies, but they were no match for what I faced."

Hiram gazed out his front window by the table. "I had a choice then, too. I could use what little power I had in hopes of getting away without harm, or I could wait until I had made it down the hill myself, lightning bolts flashing all around me as I ran. I knew if I used my weak power against Pamola, I would not survive. Nighthawk would carry me away, and I would never be seen again. But if I tried to escape Pamola, I might be able to use my power against Nighthawk who wasn't as strong."

We could see Katahdin in the distance, its sister peaks Nesourdnahunk, Soubungee, Double Top, Joe Merry, OJI and Owls Peak. These stood by themselves in a blue mass on the eastern horizon. A few clouds passed by.

"That Nighthawk spirit is a tricky one," Hiram said. "You never know if he will take you to the shadows to meet your death or just fly past on his way to another quarry. You have been lucky so far."

"Why do you think I've been lucky?"

"Nighthawk sometimes plays with his food a little first, like a cat plays with a mouse before killing it. Might have nothing to do with luck." That made some sense. Several times Nighthawk had an opportunity to take me, but hadn't. "Nighthawk knows you have power even though when you first saw him, you didn't know you had it. So, he stayed at a distance."

"Do you think he always will?" I wondered.

"He might," Hiram said. "You are from a long line of powerful shamans and chiefs with great powers, Charlie who is a Neptune. Nighthawk would be wise to leave you alone."

Hiram was the kind of human who touched the earth gently. Everything he did had a spiritual purpose. His face showed kindness. Hiram was the best teacher a young shaman could have.

Chapter 31

Father was ferrying supplies to the depots one early August morning, and I had a new task. Twenty horses had to be transported to the Grant Farm from Gero. There were nearly 200 summering on the island across the lake in a huge field, and 100 in the fields around the hotel. After the first snows came, their vacation would end, and they would return to haul spruce pulp to the landings. Two men watched over them on the island, getting hay down from the mow in the large barn, being sure the springs were clear for drinking, and keeping a watch for bears and mountain cats. We looked after the heard in back of our barn.

Horses destined for the Grant Farm were brought over on a covered barge and put in our pen. My job was to walk them twenty miles to the Grant Farm by the Deer Pond trace, not much of a road in the summer, but passable by horse. Abby came with me. We were going to bring back the mail. With ropes around the horses' necks, one tied to the next in front, we started out.

Uncle Amos, Louis and Tommy were working the stills. Father said he was close to finding a new buyer. The next few batches of Tanglefoot were ready to bottle, and more oak barrels had been filled to age. With Father away ferrying men and supplies, they saw an opportunity to escape the barn once bottling was done. The perch were still biting pretty hard, and Uncle Amos and Louis walked to the spring hole on the side of the river to see what they could catch. Tommy stayed behind to help Mother move some furniture on the top floor.

With the horses safely pastured at the Grant Farm, Abby and I rode back on Duke. She shared the back part of the saddle. It was long enough for the two of us. We walked a bit to rest Duke, but we made it to the Deer Pond camps in good time. No one had come our way, and the late afternoon stayed cool.

I was having a little trouble with Duke on the way back. Something seemed to be bothering him. Mother understood Duke, as he was the horse she often rode if she had an errand at the other end of the Village.

"I wish Mother was here," I complained. "She'd know what was upsetting him."

"Why?" Abby asked. "She's one of those horse whisperers?"

"I don't know," I sighed. "I wish he'd relax a bit."

"Let's take a rest," Abby said. "We'll check his saddle." We took a late lunch break in a little glen after we crossed Deer Pond Stream. There was a nice breeze to keep the flies away. We were packing up the remains of our lunch when Duke began to snort. It wasn't long before he was dancing around a little. Something was making him skittish. Then we began to hear something coming our way from the Village.

I got out my new shotgun and loaded two shells. I was expecting to see a hungry bear or a catamount heading our way. The over and under Winchester that I had just bought could blow a hole through any critter, even a man, if needed.

After a few minutes, the noise became horses walking and men talking. I lowered the barrel but kept the shotgun in my hands as two men in derby hats rode into the clearing.

"You planning to shoot that thing?" the first one asked, moving his hand to his side. I could see a small bulge there under his coat.

"Not unless you're a catamount or a bear," I said, lowering my weapon. "Don't look like either one from here," and I put the shotgun back in its sleeve by the saddle's horn, pocketing the shells before I did.

They tipped their hats to Abby and rode out of the clearing. "Not real chatty, were they?" Abby commented.

"Don't like that," I said.

"What?" she asked.

"Strangers like that riding through. Know who they were? Didn't look like any Company men I've seen before," I offered. "They're dressed like they just got off the boat from Boston." As soon as I said 'Boston' I became more concerned, thinking of the two thugs who had paid us a visit not too long ago washing up on the sandy shore of the lake by Blake's logging camps. There was a strong resemblance in how they were dressed.

"No, I haven't seen them before either. Maybe my dad hired

some new team bosses and they were here to check things out."

"Maybe," I said, and we continued our trek to Cunningham Brook. As we came into another clearing, I could see that the blueberries were ripening early this year. The end of June and the first of this month had been dry and hot. We had a little rain shower from time to time, just enough for the berries to stay juicy. Mother might have a wild berry pie cooling on the windowsill when we got back. I could almost smell it.

When we crossed Cunningham Bridge, Duke's nostrils flared. I smelled smoke. Abby did, too. The smell was getting stronger, and in another half-hour we could see a black plume above the pointed firs in the distance. When we were two miles from home, the wind from the north brought the smoke right to us. Duke could handle a little trot even with both of us on his back, so we hurried to see what the smoke was all about. I didn't like it. My stomach began to tighten up as we got closer. I thought I could smell burning tar-paper. Abby held her arms tight around my waist, and that helped me keep my anxiety under control.

The smell of smoke was even stronger as we turned the corner and rode down the slight grade to the hotel. There, where our home had stood, were two bare chimneys and a gaping pit where the hotel had stood. Smoke was still rising in wisps here and there. We hopped off Duke, just dropping the reins as we came to the lilac tree that Mother carefully pruned each March.

Father was standing there beside Louis and Uncle Amos. Hiram was there, too. Streaks from tears were on their faces, including Father's.

"What happened?" I almost shouted. I looked around the group staring at the smoking embers. No one spoke. Our home was gone. Only sadness looked at me from the smoking remains.

"Where's Mother? Where's Tommy?" I begged. Father opened his hand to show me a blackened locket. It was the one Mother always wore. "It was her favorite. She wore it all the time. She's gone, Charlie." He put his arm around my shoulders, a fresh tear streaking his cheek. It was the only time I saw him cry.

"We saw two men ride off, heading south," Uncle Amos reported, "just as we got back from fishing. They looked like a couple of city slickers, that's for sure. When we got back, flames were coming from the roof and some of the windows. Mother was trapped on the second floor. She was crying for help."

We could see that Tommy was with her," Louis said. "He threw a chair through the window and they had just dropped a string of sheets down, but neither of them came to the window again. I think the smoke got to them."

"Oh no, no, no," I sobbed. "It can't be." Abby put her arm around me as we stood staring at the smoking remains of our home as if it were a bad dream and everything would be back to normal after we just closed and reopened our eyes. I could feel a tingling on the back of my neck and up my scalp just like before when those men drowned in that gale. I couldn't seem to stop sobbing.

A south wind began to rise, blowing ashes and some sparks from the smoldering remains of our home. Waves on the lake rose, and I could hear a tree snap in the distance. Abby hugged me, whispering, "Charlie, you have to stop this. It's not what Mother would want." It took a moment for me to focus on Abby's voice, and as I did, the wind began to die down. After a few minutes, it was nearly calm again. No one else had heard what Abby said to me, but I could tell from the way Louis, Uncle Amos and especially Father looked at me that they knew I had brought up the wind.

I made Abby promise to say nothing about the two men who passed us at Deer Pond Stream where we were having our lunch. I thought they were up to no good, but I no idea what they had done. I didn't want Father to make things worse by taking revenge on some faceless thugs. The cycle of violence had to stop, and it had to stop now.

The next morning when the ashes had cooled, Hiram brought by two infant coffins he had made. Father and Uncle Amos looked for remains but found nothing more than a few pieces of bone. The fire had been that hot. We were amazed the locket had survived. Maybe it was the Great Spirit telling us Mother had really gone. Hiram found a few more fragments of bone that might have been Tommy's, but no one really knew.

We laid them to rest in the King family plot where we had buried William. On Mother's wooden cross the inscription read, "As you are now, so was I. As I am now, so you will be." Mother's friends joined us for the burial. We had a gathering in the church afterward. Most of the Village came.

After a brief stay with friends nearby, Father, Uncle Amos and I moved into the vacant inn near the point. A few days after the services, Father and Uncle Amos were having coffee at the kitchen table. I was cleaning up at the sink.

"You know, Caleb, this inn might be a good place to open up your own business. I think you could buy it for a good price." Uncle Amos dumped more sugar in his mug. "It'd be a good way to make some money."

"Problem is, Amos, there isn't any money to buy it with," Father replied.

"What do you mean? What about all our money from the business? Why don't you use that?"

"I can't," Father sighed, holding his head in his hands. He then looked right at his brother. "There isn't any money."

"What?" Uncle Amos cried out. I turned around from drying the last dish. "I thought we had over seventy grand stashed away."

"We did." Father poured himself another cup of coffee. "But it's all gone now."

"What happened to it?" I asked quietly. Father didn't seem angry, just beaten, exhausted, and downhearted.

"It was all in the strongbox I kept under the floorboards in our bedroom," Father explained. "It's all ashes now. That strongbox was supposed to be fireproof. When I dug it out of the cellar hole, there were only ashes inside."

All the risk, all the work, more than twenty lives, and only a few wooden crosses marked "Unknown" to show for it. My mother, my best friend, the only photos of Will and Sam were part of the price.

Uncle Amos slowly put down his mug. "Got any of that aged whiskey left? I think I need a drink. Or several."

I left them sitting quietly at the table, grabbed my coat and walked up to the church. There was no one around. I said some prayers for Mother and Tommy, wiped the tears from my eyes and walked up the little rise in back to the cemetery. I first came to Tommy's cross. Beside it was his brother William's, two British brothers resting side by side in a foreign land. At least their graves were marked. My own brothers were under the sod of a farmer's field in France. They had no markers. Whenever I visited our cemetery on the hill and looked at Tommy and William's graves, I imagined they were Will and Sam's, home at last. In a strange way, that thought gave me some comfort, but I still struggle with a small truth behind it all. Death is always beside us, quietly waiting, hiding in the shadows. I became determined to enjoy every sunny day, every rainy afternoon and all the bitterly cold winter mornings while I could. The beauty around us, this one fleeting thing, was all any of us really knew.

By the next spring, in spite of all that had happened, there was a new stock of Tanglefoot in the barn, waiting for a suitable buyer. Father and Amos decided to start all over. Some lessons are never learned.

That winter was the longest I remember. It was as if a strong wind had blown away any happiness I had. My best friend was gone. I would never see my mother again. Abby went to Bangor with her father until spring. They'd return when the drive started up the first of May. Even Hiram had left to run his trap lines. I never felt so very much alone.

Ki'kwa'jenu stayed in the shadows. I didn't see him at all that winter, nor did I have dreams of a creature with bright red eyes waiting for me.

Epilogue

July 1955

Gull Island had nearly disappeared in a white curtain of rain that was crawling up the lake just ahead of the storm's forward edge where the whitecaps grew higher and sharper. Under gray skies, bottoms of darker clouds close to the water and ahead of them, the waves washing over the dock made the raft disappear from swell to swell. A runabout with a green '52 Johnson 25, was clamped to the stern. The boat bobbed beside the dock on the leeward side. Mist had begun to form, and if you looked carefully with a spy glass, you could see the rain hitting the lake surface about a mile down Chesuncook Lake. It was heading our way.

Using my Bushnell's, I could see Father's *Hunky Dory* just ahead of the approaching front. The swells were high as they often are when the wind pushes up from the south. Towed behind was a string of six green canvas canoes, tied nose to tail, bobbing along in the swells. Soon, he'd be able to tie to the dock and unload the mail and cargo. The Camp Kennesuncook crew would take care of the string of canoes as soon as he tied up. I'd help him secure the boat, a job I'd been doing since I was a kid. I liked to meet him at the dock on his return trip with the mail even after thirty years. Father was just over seventy, and sometimes he had a hard time moving fast enough to tie the boat safely, rough seas or not. His balance wasn't always the best. I watched for him on his return run with the mail three days a week when I wasn't plying my own trade moving human cargo across the Canadian border. He had given me life, he had saved my life, and I felt I owed him even now. He lived alone, not so much by choice.

The spring after Mother and Tommy died in the fire, Father

161

remarried. Olive was part Penobscot. She had lived in the smaller village on Gero. She was a wonderful cook and was determined to teach me and Abby how to cook for the houseful of boarders who stayed in our Katahdin View Inn on Graveyard Point. They seemed a good match for one another, as long as Olive didn't contradict Father too often. They had nearly twenty years of happiness together. Then Olive passed away, leaving Father alone again in his little camp on the ledge facing Katahdin.

The canoes he towed up the lake belonged to Camp Kennesuncook, a boy's camp started by Father Murray from Rhode Island. Each year, he'd bring up a dozen boys from the city there. Providing their own guides, the group would paddle the Allagash, climb Mt. Katahdin, and learn how to survive in the great north woods.

After Father untied the canoes from *Hunky*, there would be just seconds for the camp's two guides to get the them safely on shore before the waves trashed them on the slippery, sharp rocks. A few older camp kids stood ready to guide them quickly and safely to shore.

Father often had a group of village kids on board for the return trip down the lake as *Hunky* ferried supplies and passengers. He'd been doing this for over forty years now. For a free ride, which they dearly loved, and hours away from parental supervision, these youngsters provided free labor. Most were strong enough to muscle the cargo aboard the boat. They could handle anything except for the occasional goat or crate of piglets, and they were good company as well.

A few years ago, when I was with him for a ride to the Dam, he took *Hunky* with his young crew of helpers over to the Cuxabexis Thoroughfare. I don't know why he did this, and I didn't need that scab ripped off again, but when we reached the thoroughfare, Father cut the old Dodge engine and drifted to a stop. "This is where it happened," he told them, and he then retold the details of that late November night in 1920. He had never spoken about it before, and he never would again, not to friends and not to family. I had a hard time hearing it, tears for those lost immigrant souls, tears for my brothers, and tears for my loving mother and Tommy momentarily blinding me. The hardest realization for me, and it was something I felt thirty-five years ago, was that our smuggling was behind all of our miseries. If only I could use my power to bring her back. I had forgiven Father years ago. I think Father had forgiven himself, too. He didn't seem to be as stern now as he was then. I think he realized that there were forces he could unleash but not command.

The dock where Father planned to land was a floating collection of old boom logs, chained and spiked together, and then planked over in places so feet didn't get soaked going from one end to the other in rough water. There were three pairs of thick planks, one pair along each side and wider planks in the middle. A two-board ramp ran from the shore to the dock's edge. Today the dock was twisting in the waves, water washing up between the logs, just another challenge for unloading.

On this afternoon, long strings of white foam were scattered over the breaking waves, pointing in the direction of the wind. When the *Hunky Dory* was securely tied up, Father's helpers got their feet wet unloading the cargo and the mail. It's not easy to walk a slippery wave-tossed and white cap washed raft of logs while carrying dunnage. Navigating the twisting, wet gang plank from dock to shore while balancing an armful of supplies is even trickier. Two grey canvas duffle bags with rope closures secured by official U.S. Post Office metal tags that read "Chesuncook Village via Greenville" held three days of mail for us 'Suncookers. These fifty-year-old mail sacks were well frayed and not at all waterproof. Sometimes letters got a little damp by the time the sack got into the P.O. for sorting.

With the *Hunky Dory* unloaded and untied, he had to back away quickly from the dock directly into the wind that had increased, and I knew we were seeing just the beginning of a bad storm on its way up to the Village.

Whenever Father left the Village, I knew that if he was not back that night, the lake was too rough. He'd just stay in his camp at the Dam. Sometimes, when there's a blow from the south, the winds howling up lower Chesuncook join those from Caribou through a narrower passage to the west. When these winds meet just off Weymouth Point, they create waves that not only tower but also crisscross. If one foam-capped peak doesn't souse you, the other will.

"Thanks, Charlie." Father stepped back in the boat. "I could use a hand tying up in the cove. Come with me?" I nodded my head.

"Good. Throw off the bow line first, then do the stern," he commanded as if I didn't know which to do first. Some things about him would never change. With the wind coming up behind him, doing it the other way around would swing the stern out into the wind, giving him no cushion for safety.

"Step aboard after you throw the stern line." Father seemed to like my company, and often filled me in on the gossip he had heard at the Dam. When he came over for supper to the Inn with me, Abby and

163

our children, I'd eat my beans and just listen.

Our kids loved to hear his stories about the moose that had charged him one fall or the giant salmon he caught. He had changed from the man he was on that cold November night in 1920 and the aftermath of the rum-running business. He seemed to listen more to Uncle Amos and Louis when they needed to straighten him out. That wasn't often, though.

As Father backed *Hunky* into the wind and away from the dock, waves splashing over the stern, temporarily silencing the exhaust as if *Hunky* was gasping for breath, he gauged the force of the wind. When the moment was right, he slammed her in forward gear, spun the wheel, and raced the engine full throttle so *Hunky* could slew around into the trough and away from the rocky, ledge covered shore. With a slight turn down wind, we motored a mile up the lake to the protected village cove where we would tie up beside the Company's steel *Boom Jumper*. As he cut back her throttle, we were both shivering from the cold wind, and I began to think of the warmth of the fireplace in the new cabin I helped him build. I miss Mother's cooking, and I know Father did, too. And I really miss her hugs. I tell her as much whenever I visit the cemetery on the hill.

With *Hunky* secured for the night, Father and I walked over the wave washed gang plank to the pebble beach and up the little rise. Ahead was the village fire station. An 8x8 whitewashed shed, it housed hoses, axes, a pump and gas. The fire shed was mostly for peace of mind. If one of the Acadian row houses along the shore caught on fire in a strong wind, they'd all go with or without Indian Pumps. Those hadn't been any help when the hotel burned.

"Come over to the inn for dinner?" I asked him. "There'll be plenty to eat, and I know you love Abby's cooking."

"Sounds good to me," Father replied, and I saw a little smile soften his hard face for just a moment. Our relationship had become easier over the years. Since Olive, my stepmother, had passed away over a decade ago, Father treated me more as a friend than a son to control. I also accepted him with all his flaws, diminished over the years.

I was glad to see my children greet him at the door, begging to hear more stories of the spirits of Katahdin and tales of river driving from the comfort of Mother's rocking chair in our kitchen. I'm telling you this story as I rock it, feeling close to her. Father never spoke about the power I had used years ago, something I had felt guilty about ever since those two men drowned. I sensed that he knew how I felt, and in turn I respected the guilt he carried for Mother's death.

As we walked down the narrow dirt road past the old cellar hole of our hotel, now overgrown by alders and birch trees poking up around the old fieldstone foundation, I glanced toward the Thoroughfare between Gero and Gull Islands. Ki'kwa'jenu was some other place tonight. I thought of that cold November night when so many trusting immigrant passengers suffered on their boat ride to the Cuxabexis logging camps. For the last thirty-five years, I have never been successful in erasing those details from my mind, try as I have. I wonder how Mother is doing in Heaven, and I try not to think about her last moments in the smoke-filled bedroom she and Father shared. On quieter nights in late November, walking home to my family, I can still hear screams from the immigrants, flowing out from unquenchable orange and yellow flames. I know Father could, too.

Glossary

Boom Chain

These chains were used to connect boom logs together. Weighing over fifty pounds, these six-foot chains had a large ring on one end and an elongated link with a trapezoid shaped toggle at the other. The toggle end was turned parallel to the chain and then passed through a three-inch hole at one end of the boom log, then straightened flat against the log and pegged in place so it would not pass through. The ring was large enough so it would not pass through the three-inch hole on the adjacent log.

Boom Log

Most were twenty feet long. A three-inch hand auger was used to cut the hole at each end. When chained together, these logs made a necklace into which were floated thousands of cords of pulp-wood. Hundreds of boom logs were used to make the necklace which was towed down the lakes to the next river corridor.

Pulp-Wood

Four-foot spruce and fir were cut during the winter and then floated down the rivers and towed down the lakes from the woods to the paper mills in Millinocket and below. This pulp wood was then ground into a mash that was pressed into different types of paper.

Boom Jumper

A steel boat, the boom jumpers had a wire cage around the propeller to protect it from damage from pulp-wood. These boats would pass over booms to navigate up river.

Long Logs

These were saw logs for lumber. Spruce, fir and pine were cut for this purpose, but pine logs were floated down the river separately. These floated lower than spruce and fir, and would often cause problems jamming up in the rapids on their way to the mills. Some were floated all the way down river some sixty miles to the saw mills in Old Town, Orono, Veazie and Bangor.

Pick Pole

Twelve to fourteen feet long, these slender poles had a metal sleeve on the end with a sharp point and sometimes a hook. Sometimes the point was threaded. The threads allowed the pole to penetrate the log enough so the river driver could push it away, and then with a simple twist of the pole, release the log. These poles were also used for balance while walking/running over a sea of floating logs, just like the pole an acrobat would use on the high wire.

Peavey

A stubby pole with a metal end, these had a hook on a hinge. The hook was driven into a log, and the handle was used like a lever to turn or move the log.

Log Jam

Wood floating down the rivers would often pile on top of each other, creating a tangled mess of pulp or long logs. River drivers had to untangle the jam, all the while watching for the logs to suddenly "haul" or start moving on their own. When that happened, they had to run for shore...fast.

Caulked Boots

These were leather boots with small spikes in the soles and heels. They made it a little safer for the river driver to keep from slipping off the log. When a river driver disappeared under a jam and drowned, his (or another pair) of boots were hung on the branch of a tree beside the spot where he went under. Today, you may see hanging from a tree a pair of sneakers from a white-water rafter who fell out (but was rescued).

Boom House

This group of buildings consisted of bunk houses for the wood cutters, a mess hall and room for the cook and cookee, a clerk's camp where the fireproof safe was kept and the day's tally slips were kept.

Depot

The depot had a large wharf with storage buildings that held supplies for all the boom houses throughout a district. Sometimes large boats were hauled out at the end of the season and kept and repaired there.

Bean Hole Beans

Beans were the staple in the woodsmen's diet. Kidney or pea beans were soaked overnight in salted water. These were dumped into a cast iron kettle that held two to three gallons of beans and pork. A pit several feet deep was dug out, and a fire was built. Using hardwood, a hot bed of coals formed. Sometimes, boom chains were put on the coals to get red-hot. This made the hole into a very hot oven. The bean pot cover was sealed up and then was lowered down into the pit, which was sealed with clay or sand. After ten to twelve hours, the cast iron pot was dug up, and the beans were served.

Chesuncook Dam

First built in 1836, the dam was washed out and rebuilt, making it higher each time. The wood and rock filled dam raised the water level about fourteen feet, flooding out Native American burial sites and many of their traditional camp sites. After it was flooded over by the construction of Rip Dam, Chesuncook Dam is still referred to as "the Dam" as a boat launching area and parking place.

Ripogenus (Rip) Dam

Completed by 1917, Rip Dam was situated over a rough set of rapids It was 100 feet high and over 700 feet long, the largest private dam in the world at the time. This dam raised the water about thirteen feet more, making Gero Island, flooding over Moose Pond, and joining Caribou and Ripogenus lakes.

Chesuncook Village

Home to sixty or so cabins and frame houses, the village today has three or four year-round residents. The summer population can be as high as seventy-five during the first two weeks of August.

Thoreau Seekers

Henry David Thoreau first visited the area in the late 1850's. By then, all the huge pines had been cut for lumber. Groups of campers paddle down the river from Northeast Carry's Roll Dam or start lower down at Hannibal's Crossing at the outflow of Lobster Lake. They camp on the river one night and then land on Gero Island or one of the other sites around the upper lake. After a visit to the church and cemetery, they paddle down the lake to the Dam with one more overnight stay. The Maine woods are much different now. Clear cutting, taking of all trees, has come within 100 feet of the river, giving the illusion of being in a heavily wooded forest.

References

Abenaki Language and culture:

        http://www.cowasuck.org/language/language.htm

        http://www.nedoba.org/index.html

Eckstorm, Fanny Hardy; The Penobscot Man; Jordan Frost, 1904

Whitehead, Ruth Holmes; Six Micmac Stories; Nimbus Publishing; 1989

Smith, Marion Whitney; Katahdin Fantasies; Millinocket Press, 1953

Smith, Marion Whitney; Strange Tales of Abenaki Shamanism; Millinocket Town Library, 1963

Wood, Richard G.; A History of Lumbering in Maine, 1820-1861; University of Maine Press, 1971

Pauling, Michal A.; Wabnaki Homeland and the New State of Maine; University of Massachusetts Press, 2007

Glaster, Charles H.; The West Brancher; Vantage Press, 1970

About the Author

B.W. Edwards spent summers at Chesuncook Village as a child. He lives and writes in Northern New England.